BUZZING WITH PURPOSE THE ART AND SCIENCE OF BEEKEEPING

by

Ivette Smith

BUZZING WITH PURPOSE THE ART AND SCIENCE OF BEEKEEPING

Paperback ISBN: 978-1-969775-89-5

Table of Contents

Introduction

As a young girl, I was captivated by the gentle hum of bees in my grandfather's backyard. The neat rows of wooden hives, the sweet scent of honey combined with the smoker in the air, and the sight of my grandfather and uncle tending to these tiny, industrious creatures sparked a fascination that would shape my life. Little did I know then that the lessons I learned at their side would teach me the art of beekeeping and instill in me a deep appreciation for the delicate balance of nature.

In recent years, garden beekeeping has surged in popularity, attracting individuals from all walks of life who seek a meaningful connection with the natural world. This resurgence is not merely a trend but a reflection of our growing awareness of bees' vital role in our ecosystems. By taking up the mantle of backyard beekeeping, we reap the sweet rewards of fresh, homegrown honey and contribute to preserving these essential pollinators.

"Buzzing with Purpose: The Art and Science of Beekeeping" is a guidebook designed to empower you, whether you're an adult, young adult, hobbyist, or gardener, with the knowledge and skills necessary to create and maintain a thriving backyard apiary. Through the pages of this book, I aim to share the insider techniques and sustainable practices that I have honed over years of beekeeping, enabling you to enhance your hive's productivity while positively impacting the ecosystem.

Within these pages, you'll find information tailored specifically for the aspiring backyard beekeeper. From understanding the fascinating world of bee biology to setting up your first hive, this book provides a comprehensive roadmap for your beekeeping journey. You'll discover expert tips on hive management, pest control, and honey harvesting, all presented in an accessible and engaging manner.

But this book is more than just a collection of practical advice. It is a testament to the transformative power of beekeeping. As you nurture your hives and witness the incredible work of these tiny creatures, you'll develop a deeper appreciation for the intricate web of life surrounding us. You'll learn how your actions, no matter how small, can profoundly impact our planet's health and resilience.

Throughout the book, we'll explore the art and science of beekeeping, from the basics of hive construction to advanced techniques for maximizing honey production. Each chapter builds upon the last, guiding you through the seasons of beekeeping and equipping you with the tools and knowledge needed to overcome challenges and celebrate successes.

As we embark on this journey together, I invite you to embrace the role of a backyard beekeeper with enthusiasm and dedication. The rewards of this practice extend far beyond the sweetness of fresh honey. By creating a haven for bees in your garden, you become a steward of the environment, contributing to the preservation of biodiversity and the health of our planet.

So, let us venture into the captivating world of beekeeping, armed with the knowledge, skills, and passion needed to make a difference. Together, we can create a future where the gentle buzz of bees continues to grace our gardens, reminding us of the beauty and resilience of the natural world.

Chapter 1: The Foundations of Garden Beekeeping

As a child, the world of bees buzzed vividly around me, thanks to my grandfather's sprawling garden and profound wisdom. He often spoke of bees as nature's architects, tirelessly working to build and sustain their colonies. Each hive was a universe governed by unique rules and roles. Watching him and my uncle tend to the hives; I learned that bees weren't just fascinating creatures—they were essential to the health of our environment. This chapter will guide you through the foundational elements of beekeeping, starting with understanding bees' intricate social structure and behavior, which is crucial for any aspiring beekeeper.

Understanding Bee Behavior

The social structure of a bee colony is a marvel of nature, where each bee has a specific role that contributes to the overall health and productivity of the hive. At the heart of the hive lies the queen bee, the central figure responsible for reproduction. Her primary duty is to lay eggs, ensuring the continuity and growth of the colony. She can lay up to 2,000 eggs per day, a feat that underscores her significance. All female workers are the unsung heroes, adept at multitasking. They forage for nectar and pollen, maintain the hive, care for the young, and protect the colony from threats. Their tireless work sustains the hive, making them indispensable. Drones, the male bees, have a singular purpose: to mate with a queen. While they do not partake in foraging or hive maintenance, their role is crucial for genetic diversity and the continuation of bee lineages.

Communication within a hive is a sophisticated dance of pheromones and movements. Bees use pheromones, chemical signals, to convey a range of messages, from alerting others to danger to regulating the hive's social structure. The "waggle dance," a term that might sound whimsical, is an exact form of communication. It's a dance performed by forager bees to inform their hive mates about the location of food sources. The angle and duration of the dance encode information about the direction and distance relative to the sun. This intricate dance is learned through social interactions, highlighting the importance of experienced bees in educating the young, much like social learning observed in humans.

The lifecycle of a bee is a testament to nature's efficiency, transforming from egg to adult in a matter of weeks. It begins with the egg stage, which lasts about three days. The egg hatches into a larva, resembling a tiny, white grub. During this stage, which lasts about six days, the nurse bees feed the larva royal jelly, pollen, and honey. Afterward, the larva spins a cocoon and enters the pupa stage, undergoing metamorphosis. Within this cell, it transforms into an adult bee, emerging ready to fulfill its role in the hive. From egg to adult, this cycle takes about 21 days for worker bees, slightly longer for drones, and shorter for queens.

Bee behavior is also highly responsive to environmental changes, showcasing their adaptability. One of the most dramatic behaviors is swarming, a natural process of colony reproduction. When a hive becomes overcrowded, or resources are abundant, a queen and a large group of bees will leave to establish a new colony. This process, while natural, can be managed through regular hive inspections and maintenance. Another behavior, known as bearding, occurs in response to heat. When temperatures rise, bees gather outside the hive to cool it down, resembling a "beard" hanging from the hive entrance. Understanding these behaviors allows beekeepers to anticipate and respond effectively to the needs of their colonies, ensuring their survival and productivity.

Here's a breakdown of the different types of bees in a colony and their roles: Queen

- **Appearance:**
    - Larger than worker bees with an elongated abdomen.
    - Smooth, shiny back (less hairy than workers).
    - Moves more slowly and is often surrounded by worker bees.

Key Facts:

✅ Lays up to 2,000 eggs per day.

✅ Releases pheromones that regulate the hive's behavior.

✅ Typically lives 2–5 years (longest lifespan in the colony).

🐝 2. Worker Bees (Females) 💪

- **Role:** Perform all tasks except laying eggs.
- **Appearance:**
    - Smaller than the queen.
    - Fuzzy bodies with pollen baskets on their hind legs.
    - Slightly different in size depending on their job.
- **Lifecycle & Duties:**

🐣 **Days 1–3:** Clean the hive and cells.

🍼 **Days 4–10:** Feed larvae and tend to the queen.

🏗️ **Days 11–20:** Build comb, store food, and guard the hive.

✈ **Days 21+:** Become foragers, collecting nectar, pollen, water, and propolis.

Key Facts:

- ✅ Short lifespan (4–6 weeks in summer, up to 6 months in winter).

- ✅ Can sting to protect the hive but dies afterward.

- ✅ Produce wax for honeycomb construction.

🐝 3. Drone Bees (Males) 🐝

- **Role:** Mate with a queen from another colony.

- **Appearance:**

  - Larger and bulkier than workers but smaller than the queen.

  - Big eyes for spotting queens during mating flights.

  - No stinger and no pollen baskets.

Key Facts:

- ✅ Do not collect food or help in the hive.

- ✅ Their only purpose is to **mate with a queen**, then they die.

- ✅ Expelled from the hive before winter to conserve resources.

Reflection: Observing Bee Behavior take a moment to observe your hive. Note any signs of swarming or bearding. How do the bees communicate with one another? Reflect on how the social structure of the hive influences these behaviors.

This foundational knowledge empowers you to navigate the complexities of beekeeping with confidence, linking the rhythms of your hive to the broader tapestry of nature.

Essential Equipment for the Urban Apiary

A thriving urban apiary begins with gathering the right tools and equipment. Like a carpenter relies on a trusted set of tools, a beekeeper needs a reliable array of gear to ensure safety and productivity. You'll find the brood box, supers, and frames at the heart of your setup—key hive components. The brood box serves as the bee's living quarters, where the queen lays eggs and young bees develop. Above it, the supers are stacked to store the honey that the bees produce and for you to harvest. Inside each box, frames hang vertically, providing a structure upon which bees build their comb. Together, these elements form the foundation of your hive, a carefully designed space that mimics the natural habitat bees need to thrive in.

Protective gear is just as crucial, ensuring your safe and enjoyable beekeeping experience. A well-fitted beekeeping suit with gloves and a protective veil acts as your armor against potentially painful bee stings. These suits are designed to be both breathable and durable, offering protection without causing discomfort. The gloves must allow for dexterity, enabling you to handle the hive components precisely. The veil protects your face and neck—areas most vulnerable to stings—while maintaining visibility. Investing in quality protective gear is not just about comfort; it is about ensuring safety during every hive inspection and maintenance task.

When selecting equipment, the importance of quality cannot be overstressed. Durable materials not only withstand the test of time but also reduce the likelihood of unexpected failures that could jeopardize your bees' well-being. Inferior equipment may require frequent repairs and replacements, leading to unnecessary expenses and frustration. Quality equipment, on the other hand, offers peace of mind, allowing you to focus on nurturing your colony rather than constantly troubleshooting hardware issues. Addressing this is particularly vital in urban settings where space is often limited, and the opportunity for intervention is less frequent.

Urban beekeeping presents unique challenges, and having the right location-specific tools can make all the difference. Smokers, for instance, are indispensable for calming bees during hive inspections. They work by masking alarm pheromones, helping to maintain a peaceful atmosphere within the hive. Hive tools resemble small crowbars and are essential for prying apart frames and scraping off excess wax or propolis. These tools are designed to be multifunctional, providing the flexibility needed to navigate the constraints of urban spaces.

Maintaining your equipment is a practice that cannot be overlooked. Regular inspections for wear and tear ensure that both the hive and your gear remain in optimal condition. Cleaning protocols are crucial, particularly for hive tools, which can become breeding grounds for bacteria and other pathogens if neglected. After each use, clean your tools with a mild bleach solution or hot water, then dry them thoroughly to prevent rust. Proper storage, away from moisture and direct sunlight, further extends the life of your equipment, safeguarding your investment.

Practical Exercise: Equipment Checklist

Before you begin, create a checklist of all necessary tools and equipment. Include the basic hive components, protective gear, and any location-specific tools you might need. Regularly update this list as you learn and expand your apiary.

Equipping yourself with the right tools and maintaining them carefully sets the stage for successful beekeeping. It ensures you are prepared to meet the demands of your hives and the challenges of urban beekeeping with confidence, allowing your focus to remain on the bees themselves.

🐝 Urban Beekeeping Equipment List

🏠 1. Beehives

- **Langstroth Hive** (most common & modular — great for beginners)
    - 1 Deep Brood Box (or 2, depending on climate)

- Medium or shallow honey supers
- **Bottom Board** (with or without a screen for ventilation/pest control)
- **Inner Cover**
- **Outer Cover/Roof** (weatherproof)
- **Entrance Reducer** (helps control pests and drafts)

✅ Optional but useful:

- Hive stand (keeps hive off the ground/roof and helps airflow)

🧤 2. Protective Gear

- **Bee Suit or Jacket with Veil**
- **Beekeeping Gloves** (leather or ventilated fabric)
- **Boots or closed-toe shoes**

✅ *Urban tip:* Consider light, breathable materials — rooftops can get hot!

🔥 3. Hive Tools

- **Hive Tool** (for prying open boxes and lifting frames)
- **Smoker** (calms bees, makes inspections easier)
- **Fuel for smoker** (wood chips, pine needles, burlap, etc.)
- **Bee Brush** (for gently moving bees off comb)

🔍 4. Inspection & Management Tools

- **Frame Grip** (optional but helpful for lifting frames)
- **Frame Holder** (clips to side of hive for resting frames during inspection)
- **Queen Catcher or Marking Pen** (optional for identifying your queen)
- **Notebook or App** (for tracking inspections and hive health)

🧴 5. Feeding Equipment

- **Feeder** (Boardman, top feeder, or frame feeder depending on hive setup)
- **Sugar & water** (for making syrup — usually 1:1 in spring, 2:1 in fall)

🐿 6. Pest & Disease Management

- **Screened bottom board** (for mite monitoring)
- **Varroa mite test kit** (sugar roll or alcohol wash)
- **Mite treatments** (formic acid, oxalic acid, or other approved treatments)

🍯 7. Honey Harvesting Gear (When Ready)

- **Uncapping Knife or Fork**

- **Honey Extractor** (manual or electric — can often be rented/shared)

- **Honey Filter and Bucket**

- **Bottling Equipment** (jars, labels, caps)

  ✅ *Urban tip:* Many small-scale beekeepers **crush and strain** instead of using extractors.

📦 8. Storage & Transport

- **Extra Boxes & Frames** (for expansions or splits) **Nuc Box** (for catching swarms or raising a new queen)

- **Bee Escape Board** (optional for clearing supers of bees during harvest)

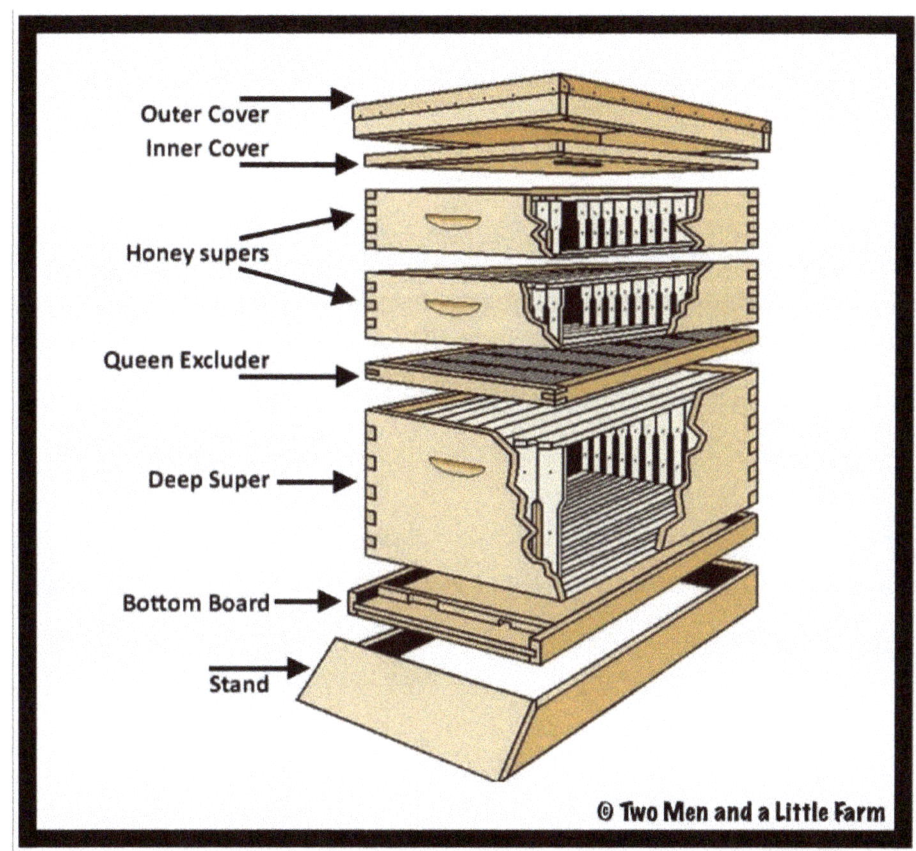

Outer Cover
Inner Cover
Honey supers
Queen Excluder
Deep Super
Bottom Board
Stand
© Two Men and a Little Farm

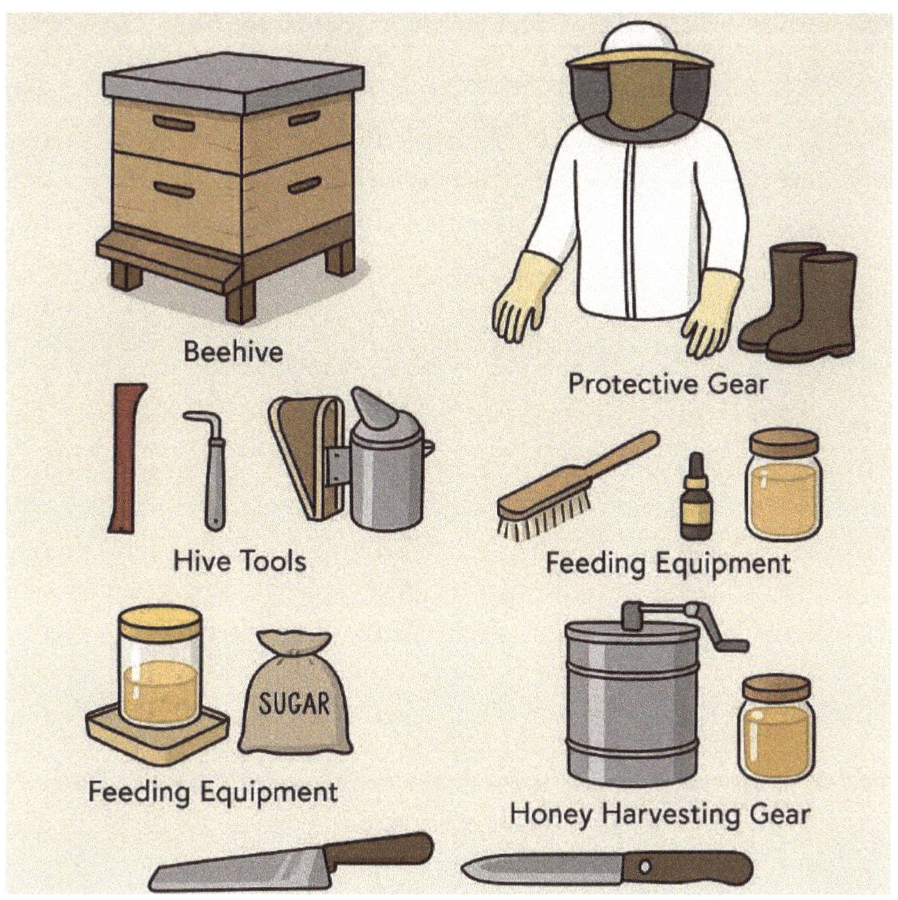

Beehive
Protective Gear
Hive Tools
Feeding Equipment
SUGAR
Feeding Equipment
Honey Harvesting Gear

🐝 Additional Setup Considerations

☀ Sunlight & Shade

- **Rooftop:** Ensure at least **6+ hours of morning sun** but provide shade for hot afternoons.
- **Backyard:** Position the hive in a **sunny spot with partial shade in the afternoon** to prevent overheating.

💨 Wind & Weather Protection

- **Rooftop:** Use a windbreak **(e.g., tall plants, fencing, or a partial enclosure).**
- **Backyard:** Place hives **near a wall, fence, or shrubs** to reduce wind exposure.

💧 Water Source

- **Provide a shallow water dish** with pebbles or floating corks for bees to land on.
- Change water regularly to prevent mosquitoes.

📏 Hive Spacing

- **Rooftop:** If keeping multiple hives, leave **2–3 feet between each** to prevent overcrowding.
- **Backyard:** Keep **at least 5 feet from walkways** and **fence off if necessary**.

    If you're **focused on honey production**, go with a **Langstroth or Flow Hive.**

    If you prefer **natural beekeeping**, a **Top-Bar or Warre Hive** is a great choice.

    For **small spaces, Flow Hives and Warre Hives** take up the least room.

Urban beekeeping has many benefits, but it also comes with challenges. Here are some key **cons** to consider:

🐝 1. Limited Foraging Resources

- Urban environments may have fewer **diverse flowers** compared to rural areas.
- Bees may rely on **ornamental plants**, which may lack nectar or be treated with pesticides.
- You may need to plant additional flowers or supplement food during dearth periods.

🚫 2. Pesticide & Pollution Exposure

- Cities often have higher levels of **air pollution**, which can affect bee health.
- Urban landscaping and agriculture often use **pesticides and herbicides** that harm bees.
- Bees may bring contaminated nectar or pollen back to the hive.

🏠 3. Neighbor Concerns & Legal Restrictions

- Not everyone is comfortable with bees; **neighbors may complain** about swarms or stings.
- Some cities require **permits, inspections, or limit hive numbers**.

- Fear of **allergic reactions** can lead to conflicts, even if bees are non-aggressive.

🌡 4. Extreme Temperature & Microclimate Challenges

- **Rooftops get very hot in summer**, which can stress bees and melt wax.
- **Concrete absorbs heat**, making urban environments warmer than rural areas.
- Some areas may have fewer **natural windbreaks or shade**, requiring artificial protection.

💧 5. Water Source Issues

- Bees may seek water from **swimming pools, pet bowls, or fountains**, causing complaints.
- You'll need to provide a **dedicated water source** close to the hive.

🚚 6. Transportation & Hive Management

- Moving equipment, honey, or new bee colonies up and down **stairs or elevators** can be a hassle.
- Hive inspections in tight spaces (rooftops, balconies, small yards) can be difficult.

🐜 7. Pest & Disease Risks

- Higher concentration of beekeepers in a city means disease and mite infestations can spread quickly.
- Limited space makes it harder to relocate or separate sick colonies.
- Urban environments may have more ants, wasps, or rodents looking for honey.

🛠 8. Hive Overpopulation & Swarming

- Too many hives in one area can lead to **competition for resources**.
- Swarming can be a concern if not managed properly, especially near residential areas.
- Some cities may have **limits on hive density** to prevent overcrowding.

⚖ 9. Lower Honey Yield Compared to Rural Areas

- Less access to **large nectar sources** means lower honey production.
- More supplemental feeding may be required, which adds to costs.

How to Overcome These Challenges?

- ✅ **Educate neighbors** and offer honey to build goodwill.
- ✅ **Choose the right location** (shade, wind protection, water source).
- ✅ **Check local regulations** before starting.
- ✅ **Plant bee-friendly flowers** to support foraging.
- ✅ **Regular hive inspections** to prevent swarming and disease spread

Setting Up Your First Hive: A Step-by-Step Guide

Establishing your first hive is a momentous occasion, one that marks the beginning of your beekeeping experience. The first step in this process is selecting the perfect location for your hive. Look for a spot that offers ample sun exposure. Bees thrive in warmth, which helps them maintain an optimal internal hive temperature. Additionally, the location should provide protection from harsh winds. A natural windbreak, such as a hedge, or a man-made barrier can shield your hive from gusts. It's also wise to consider accessibility for you, as the beekeeper, to ensure ease of maintenance and inspection.

Once you've chosen the location, the next task is to assemble your hive. Begin with a sturdy, level base to prevent any tilting or instability. This will ensure that the hive remains secure and accessible for the bees as they build their combs. Carefully construct each component: the brood box, supers, and frames. Ensure that everything fits snugly yet allows for easy manipulation during inspections. Proper assembly is crucial, as it provides the bees with a stable environment and minimizes the risk of unwanted intrusions from pests.

The initial hive inspection is a critical step after installation. It serves as your first opportunity to assess the health and well-being of your colony. During this inspection, check for the presence of the queen. Her presence is vital as she lays the eggs necessary for the colony's expansion. Look for a solid brood pattern, which indicates a healthy queen and thriving colony. Also, keep an eye out for signs of disease or pest infestations. Early detection can prevent small issues from escalating into major problems. This first inspection sets the tone for future interactions with your hive, so take your time and observe carefully.

Introducing bees to their new home is a delicate process that requires patience and care. When transferring bees, aim to minimize stress. Gently pour or brush them into the hive, maintaining calm movements to avoid agitation. It's a good idea to perform this transfer in the late afternoon or early evening when the bees are less active. Once inside, monitor the hive for signs of settling. You should see bees orienting themselves to their new environment, exploring the entrance, and organizing the interior. This settling activity is a positive sign that your bees are acclimating well.

After the initial setup, immediate post-setup maintenance is essential for hive stability. Providing supplementary feeding options, such as sugar syrup or pollen patties, can support your colony as they establish themselves. This is especially important if natural forage is limited. Regularly monitor the hive for activity, noting the level of foraging and the presence of pollen stores. Consistent observation helps you gauge the colony's progress and identify any potential issues early on. Maintaining a stable environment during these first few weeks is crucial for the long-term success of your hive.

As you undertake this process, remember that beekeeping is as much about observation and learning as it is about action. Each step you take, from selecting the location to monitoring hive activity, contributes to the overall health and productivity of your bees. Embrace the rhythms of your hive and let them guide your actions. In doing so, you cultivate not only a thriving colony but also a deeper connection with the natural world. This connection, born from dedication and care, enriches your life and supports the broader ecological community. Your hive represents a small, yet significant, contribution to the web of life that sustains us all.

Effective Hive Ventilation Techniques

Proper ventilation in a beehive is as crucial as the air we breathe. It directly impacts the health and productivity of your bees. Without adequate airflow, moisture builds up inside the hive, creating a damp environment conducive to mold and mildew. These conditions can weaken bees and lead to the spread of diseases. Moreover, poor ventilation can cause temperature fluctuations that stress the colony. Bees work tirelessly to maintain a stable environment, and when ventilation is lacking, their energy diverts from honey production to climate control. Ensuring your hive has proper ventilation supports your bees' natural processes and boosts their efficiency.

To enhance airflow within your hive, consider several practical solutions that cater to the specific needs of your environment and hive design. Start by ensuring that your hive is elevated off the ground. This simple step prevents moisture from seeping in and allows air to circulate beneath the hive. A screened bottom board can further improve ventilation by facilitating airflow through the base of the hive while also helping with mite control. Additionally, propping open the inner cover with small sticks or spacers can create an upper entrance for air to flow in and out, reducing humidity levels inside. These modifications work together to create a more breathable atmosphere for your bees.

Hive design plays a significant role in ventilation efficiency, so it's worth considering how different structures impact airflow. Langstroth hives, with their removable frames and modular design, allow for easy adjustments to enhance ventilation. Top-bar hives, while less conventional, often feature sloped roofs that promote air circulation naturally. Warre hives, inspired by traditional beekeeping methods, incorporate quilt boxes and ventilation holes that facilitate airflow while maintaining warmth during colder months. Each design offers unique advantages, so choose one that aligns with your climate and beekeeping goals. Understanding how these elements interact within your hive helps create an environment where bees can thrive.

Seasonal adjustments are crucial for maintaining optimal ventilation as weather conditions change. In spring and summer, when temperatures rise and humidity increases, enhancing airflow is essential to prevent overheating. Remove entrance reducers and ensure that all ventilation openings are clear of obstructions. Consider installing a screened inner cover to facilitate air movement without compromising bee security. As fall approaches and temperatures drop, it's time to reassess ventilation needs. While airflow remains important, excessive openings can lead to heat loss. Gradually reduce ventilation openings while ensuring some airflow remains to prevent condensation buildup.

In winter, bees cluster together to generate warmth, making it imperative to strike a balance between insulation and ventilation. Use an insulated quilt board or moisture-absorbing materials like burlap or wood shavings above the inner cover to capture excess moisture while retaining heat. Ensure that your hive has a small upper entrance for stale air to escape without letting cold drafts in. Regularly check for signs of condensation during warmer winter days and adjust ventilation as needed to maintain a dry interior environment. These seasonal adaptations ensure that your hive remains a stable haven for bees year-round.

By understanding the importance of effective hive ventilation and implementing these techniques, you provide your bees with an environment that supports their natural behaviors and maximizes their productivity. Balancing airflow with insulation requires thoughtful adjustments and ongoing observation. The reward is a healthy colony capable of thriving through seasonal variations, producing honey and pollinating plants in your garden and beyond. As you continue refining your approach, remember that each decision you make contributes to the well-being of your bees and the broader ecosystem they support.

Choosing the Right Bees for Your Climate

Selecting the right type of bees for your specific climate is one of the most crucial decisions you'll make as a beekeeper. Local weather patterns, including temperature fluctuations and humidity levels, play a significant role in the health and productivity of your bees. In regions with hot, humid summers, bees need to be resilient to high temperatures and capable of managing moisture within the hive. Conversely, in colder climates, bees must be able to withstand long periods of cold and navigate the challenges of limited winter forage. Understanding these environmental factors helps ensure that your bees not only survive but thrive, producing ample honey and contributing positively to local ecosystems.

Among the common bee species, Italian and Russian bees offer unique traits that make them suitable for different climates. Italian bees, known for their gentle demeanor and robust honey production, are a popular choice in moderate climates. They are highly productive and maintain large colonies, which can be advantageous for maximizing honey yield. However, their tendency to keep a large brood area can lead to early winter starvation if not carefully managed. On the other hand, Russian bees are renowned for their hardiness and disease resistance, especially against varroa and tracheal mites. These traits make them well-suited for harsher climates, where their ability to regulate brood production based on pollen availability is beneficial. Their natural resistance and adaptability can reduce the need for chemical interventions, aligning well with sustainable beekeeping practices.

When sourcing bees, you have several options to consider, each with its own set of benefits. Local bee suppliers and beekeeping associations are excellent starting points. They often provide bees that are already acclimated to the local environment, increasing the likelihood of success. Purchasing nucleus colonies, or "nucs," is another viable option. These small, established colonies come with a queen, workers, and brood, allowing for a smoother transition into your apiary. Alternatively, packaged bees offer a more cost-effective option, though they may require more time to establish. When deciding between these options, consider the specific needs of your apiary and the level of support available from local beekeeping communities.

The importance of choosing bees acclimated to your local environment cannot be overstated. Bees that are well-adapted to local conditions exhibit enhanced resilience to regional pests and diseases, reducing the need for chemical treatments and interventions. This adaptability translates to healthier colonies that can better withstand environmental stresses, such as unexpected weather changes or fluctuations in food availability. By selecting bees that are already accustomed to your climate, you are setting the stage for a more successful and sustainable beekeeping experience.

🌐 How to Choose the Right Bees for Your Climate

🔥 1. Hot & Dry Climates (Southwest US, Mediterranean, etc.)

🐝 **Best Bees:**

- **Italian Bees**
  - Gentle, good honey producers, tolerate heat well.
- **Carniolan Bees**
  - Handle temperature swings well, conserve resources in droughts.

  ✅ *Tip:* Choose bees that are known for *low water consumption* and strong foraging instincts.

❄️ 2. Cold & Long Winters (Northern US, Canada, Northern Europe)

🐝 **Best Bees:**

- **Carniolan Bees**
  - Cold-hardy, build up fast in spring.
- **Russian Bees**
  - Extremely winter-hardy, resistant to varroa mites.
- **Buckfast Bees**
  - Bred for northern climates; good survival in harsh winters.

  ✅ *Tip:* Look for bees that overwinter well, cluster tightly, and don't burn through honey stores.

☁ 3. Wet & Humid Climates (Pacific Northwest, UK, etc.)

🐝 Best Bees:

- **Caucasian Bees**
  - Gentle, work well in cooler, damp conditions.
- **Carniolan Bees**
  - Tolerant of moisture and variable weather.

  ⚠ Avoid breeds that are prone to robbing or don't tolerate mold and moisture well.

🏙 4. Urban/Suburban Environments (Any Climate)

🐝 Consider:

- **Gentleness is key** – avoid aggressive breeds like Africanized hybrids.
- Choose bees that are **calm around frequent human presence**.
- Avoid highly swarmy strains—space is limited in urban setups.

Top urban-friendly choices:

- Italian Bees
- Carniolan Bees
- Buckfast Bees

  ✅ *Pro tip:* Ask local beekeeping clubs which breeds are thriving in your city. Locally adapted bees often perform best

Resource List: Local Bee Suppliers and Associations

Research local bee suppliers and associations in your area. Compile a list of contacts and resources that can support your beekeeping endeavors. This network will prove invaluable as you establish and grow your apiary.

📦 Where to Get Your Bees

- **Nucleus colonies (nucs)** – mini hives with a queen, brood, and workers
- **Bee packages** – a box of bees and a caged queen
- **Local splits or swarms** – often better adapted to your climate

As you make these decisions, keep in mind that the health and productivity of your bees are intertwined with the environment in which they exist. By carefully considering your regional climate, the characteristics of different bee species, and the source of your bees, you are laying the foundation for a thriving and resilient apiary. Each choice you make in this process carries the potential to impact not only your hives but also the broader ecosystem that your bees will support through their pollination activities.

Chapter 2: Hive Management Essentials

As a child, I remember the buzz of activity around the hives on my family's property, but it wasn't just the bees at work. My grandfather often commented on the unseen threats lurking within—a shadow over the otherwise harmonious hum.

Seasonal Hive Inspections: What to Look For

Each season paints a different picture inside your hive, and understanding these changes is key to maintaining a thriving colony. In the spring, your primary goal is to assess colony strength and ensure the queen is actively laying eggs. A robust population is crucial as the hive prepares for the nectar flow. Look for healthy brood patterns, which indicate a productive queen. Observe pollen stores and honey reserves. Spring is a time of renewal, and your hive should bustle with activity as bees forage and expand their brood nest.

As summer unfolds, inspections shift to maintaining balance within the hive. With the influx of nectar, your bees will be busy filling honey supers. It's vital to prevent overcrowding by adding additional boxes as needed. Inspect for signs of swarming, such as queen cells or increased bee activity outside the hive. The hive should be buzzing with energy, and a strong honey flow will keep your bees engaged and productive. Monitor for signs of pests or diseases, as warm weather can exacerbate these issues.

Autumn brings a different set of challenges as you prepare your hive for the colder months ahead. The focus shifts to ensuring adequate food stores for winter survival. Check honey reserves and consider supplemental feeding if necessary. Inspect for pests that might weaken the hive over winter. Reduce entrance size to help the hive conserve heat and prevent robbing by other bees or pests. The goal is to fortify your colony, creating a strong, healthy population that can endure the winter months.

Winter inspections are less frequent due to cold temperatures but remain essential. Your primary concern is ensuring the hive has enough honey to sustain it through the season. On warmer days, inspect briefly to check for moisture accumulation inside the hive. Moisture can be more detrimental than cold, so ensure proper ventilation to reduce condensation. Observe bee activity at the entrance on mild days; a gentle hum indicates the colony is alive and well.

During inspections, several indicators help assess hive health. Look for solid brood patterns with minimal gaps, which suggests a healthy queen and thriving workers. Examine honey and pollen stores; adequate reserves are crucial for feeding the colony. Check for signs of disease or pests—early detection can prevent severe problems later. Notice bee behavior; calm, organized activity usually signifies a healthy hive, while erratic movements may indicate stress. Pay attention to the hive's scent; a pleasant, sweet aroma suggests good health, while sour or foul odors often signal trouble.

Efficient inspections require the right tools and techniques. A hive tool is indispensable for prying apart frames and scraping excess propolis or wax. A smoker calms bees and makes inspections smoother. Use a bee brush to gently move bees without harming them. Keep records during each inspection; note that observations help track trends and inform future management decisions. Be methodical in your approach, moving frame by frame to avoid missing critical details.

The frequency and duration of inspections vary with the seasons and your specific goals. Inspect every 7 to 10 days in spring and summer to keep pace with rapid changes in the hive. Each inspection should last about 20 to 30 minutes—long enough to be thorough but brief enough to minimize disruption. In autumn, reduce the frequency to every few weeks as the hive prepares for winter. Winter inspections are limited to warm days when bees are active; these should be quick checks lasting no more than 10 minutes.

Besides regular checks, adapt your inspection schedule based on specific needs or concerns that arise. If you suspect disease or pest issues, increase inspection frequency until resolved. Conversely, you can extend intervals between checks if everything appears stable and healthy. Consistency in monitoring allows you to respond effectively to changes within the hive, ensuring its success.

Throughout these processes, remember that beekeeping combines science and intuition. Approach each inspection with curiosity and care, observing individual elements and how they interconnect within the hive's ecosystem. Your role as a beekeeper is both steward and student, learning from the bees while guiding them through the seasons with informed decisions and responsive actions.

Varroa mites are one of the most insidious dangers to hive health. These tiny parasites can wreak havoc on a colony, attaching themselves to bees and feeding on their bodily fluids. They weaken the bees, spreading viruses and often leading to the collapse of entire colonies if left unchecked. This chapter addresses vital strategies for preventing and managing Varroa mite infestations, a cornerstone of successful hive management.

Preventing and Managing Varroa Mite Infestations

Varroa mites pose a significant threat to bee colonies worldwide. These parasites drain bees of vital nutrients and act as vectors for viruses that can devastate a hive. Early detection is crucial, as unchecked infestations can lead to dwindling bee populations and, ultimately, colony collapse. Symptoms like deformed wings or erratic behavior in bees often signal a mite problem. Consistent monitoring and timely intervention are key to maintaining hive health.

Integrated pest management (IPM) offers a holistic approach to controlling Varroa mites. This strategy combines biological, mechanical, and chemical methods to keep mite levels in check without relying solely on synthetic treatments. It begins with cultural practices such as maintaining strong colonies and using mite-resistant bee strains. Mechanical controls include drone brood removal, as mites prefer to reproduce in drone cells. By periodically removing these cells, you can significantly reduce mite populations. Chemical treatments should be used judiciously, opting for organic acids like formic or oxalic acid when necessary, which are less harmful to bees and the environment.

Regular monitoring of mite levels is essential for effective management. One standard method is the sugar shake test, where bees are gently shaken in powdered sugar to dislodge mites, which can then be counted against a white surface. Another method is the alcohol wash, which provides more accurate results but sacrifices some bees in the process. Monitoring should be consistent, ideally every few weeks during peak seasons when mite reproduction is high. Keeping detailed records of mite counts helps track trends and informs treatment decisions.

Timing and application of treatments play a critical role in managing mite populations effectively. Treatments are most effective when applied during periods of low brood production, as mites reproduce within brood cells. Late winter or early spring, before bees begin building up their brood nests, is an ideal time for treatment. Another critical window is late summer or early fall, after honey harvesting but before winter bees begin developing. Careful application of treatments ensures they target mites without harming bees or contaminating honey.

Interactive Element: Varroa Mite Monitoring Checklist

Create your own checklist for Varroa mite monitoring in your apiary. Include columns for date, method used (sugar shake or alcohol wash), number of mites counted, and any treatment applied. Regularly updating this checklist will help you identify patterns and make informed decisions about hive management. Interactive Element: Varroa Mite Monitoring Checklist

Create your own checklist for Varroa mite monitoring in your apiary. Include columns for date, method used (sugar shake or alcohol wash), number of mites counted, and any treatment applied. Regularly updating this checklist will help you identify patterns and make informed decisions about hive management.

Managing Varroa mites requires vigilance and adaptability. You can protect your hives from these pervasive pests by employing integrated pest management strategies, regularly monitoring them, and timing treatments effectively. Through careful observation and proactive measures, you ensure the vitality of your colonies, allowing them to thrive and continue their essential work within our ecosystems.

To determine what's inside a honeycomb, you can use visual inspection, touch, and sometimes even sound. Here's how to tell the difference between honey, pollen, and brood inside a comb

Managing Varroa mites requires vigilance and adaptability. By employing integrated pest management strategies, monitoring regularly, and timing treatments effectively, you can protect your hives from these pervasive pests. Through careful observation and proactive measures, you ensure the vitality of your colonies, allowing them to thrive and continue their essential work within our ecosystems.

To determine what's inside a honeycomb, you can use **visual inspection, touch, and sometimes even sound**. Here's how to tell the difference between honey, pollen, and brood inside a comb:

🐝 1. Honey 🍯

✅ Appearance:

- **Capped honey:** Covered with a thin layer of white or light wax.
- **Uncapped honey:** Shiny, golden, or amber liquid inside the cells.

✅ Location on the Frame:

- Usually found at the top of the frame or in an arc shape above the brood area.

✅ How to Test:

- **Tap the comb gently**—honeycomb sounds solid and dense.
- If uncapped, tilt the frame—honey may glisten or slowly drip out.
- **Poke with a tool or finger**—honey is thick and sticky.

🐝 2. Pollen (Bee Bread) 🌿

✅ Appearance:

- Cells filled with **brightly colored granules** (yellow, orange, red, purple, or brown).
- No wax cappings—left open for easy access by worker bees.

✅ Location on the Frame: Usually stored between the honey and brood area

✅ How to Test:

- Scraping lightly with a tool—pollen crumbles like chalk or clay.
- Look for **bees packing pollen into cells**—it means fresh pollen.

🐝 3. Brood (Eggs, Larvae, Pupae) 🐣

✅ Eggs & Larvae (Open Brood)

- **Eggs:** Tiny, white, rice-shaped specks at the bottom of a cell.

- **Larvae:** White, curled in a "C" shape inside an **open, wet-looking cell**.

✅ Pupae (Capped Brood)

- Capped with **tan or brown wax** (not white like honey).

- **Worker brood caps** are mostly flat.

- **Drone brood caps** are **slightly domed and larger**.

✅ Location on the Frame:

- Found in the **center of brood frames**, surrounded by pollen and honey.

✅ How to Test:

- **Gently press a capped brood cell**—it feels **firm but slightly spongy.**

- **Sunken or perforated brood caps** could indicate disease.

How to Inspect Frames Efficiently:

1. Hold the frame up to natural light – honey will glisten, while pollen and brood appear opaque.

2. Use a hive tool to lightly scrape – pollen crumbles, honey oozes, brood remains intact.

3. Observe the bees' activity – nurse bees tend brood, foragers bring pollen, and honey cells are capped by wax workers.

🔍 Step-by-Step Guide to Inspecting a Honeycomb Frame

Follow these steps to identify honey, pollen, and brood inside your honeycomb frames efficiently.

🛠️ What You Need:

✅ Beekeeping suit & gloves 🧤

✅ Hive tool 🛠️

✅ Smoker (optional) 🔥

✅ Flashlight or sunlight ☀️

✅ A gentle touch (to avoid damaging the comb)

📌 Step 1: Remove & Hold the Frame Properly

1 Gently **pry the frame loose** with a hive tool.

2 Lift it out **slowly and smoothly** to avoid squishing bees.

3 Hold the frame **at eye level**, tilting it slightly toward the light.

🐝 Step 2: Identify What's Inside the Cells

🍯 HONEY CHECK

🔍 Look for:

- **Capped honey:** White or light-colored wax covering the cells.
- **Uncapped honey:** Shiny, golden, or amber liquid inside cells.

🛠 Test:

- Tap gently—capped honey **feels firm**.
- Uncapped honey may **drip when tilted**.

📌 Where to Find It?

✅ Usually at the **top of the frame** or outer edges.

🌿 POLLEN (BEE BREAD) CHECK

🔍 Look for:

- **Colorful granules** in open cells—yellow, orange, red, brown, or purple.
- A **slightly moist or shiny surface** (if fermented).

🛠 Test:

- Scrape lightly—pollen **crumbles like chalk or clay.**

📌 Where to Find It?

✅ Stored between the honey and brood area, forming a band.

🐣 BROOD CHECK (Eggs, Larvae, Pupae)

Eggs & Larvae (Open Brood) 🍼

🔍 Look for:

- **Eggs:** Tiny, white, rice-shaped specks at the bottom of a cell.
- **Larvae:** White, curled in a "C" shape, floating in royal jelly.

🛠 Test:

- Use **sunlight or a flashlight**—eggs are very small and easier to see with light.

📌 Where to Find It?

✅ In the **center of brood frames**, surrounded by pollen.

Pupae (Capped Brood) 🏠

🔍 Look for:

- **Flat, tan, or brown wax caps** over cells (NOT white like honey).
- **Drone brood caps** are **more domed**, while **worker brood caps** are flatter.

🔧 Test:

- Gently **press a capped brood cell**—it should feel **slightly spongy.**
- If the caps look **sunken or perforated**, check for disease.

📌 Where to Find It?

✅ Mostly in the **center of the frame** with a mix of eggs, larvae, and pupae.

🔔 Step 3: Watch for Signs of Hive Health

✅ Healthy signs:

- White wax cappings over honey
- Brightly colored pollen
- Evenly capped brood with no gaps (good laying pattern)

🔔 Warning signs:

- Sunken or discolored brood caps (possible disease)
- Excessive gaps in brood (queen issues)
- Moldy or foul-smelling pollen (moisture problem)

🔄 Step 4: Return the Frame to the Hive

1 **Lower the frame gently** back into its slot.

2 Ensure **bees have space** before sliding frames together.

3 Close the hive carefully to avoid crushing bees.

✅ Pro Tip: Take Notes!

Keep a **hive inspection journal** to track what you see. This helps monitor honey stores, brood health, and potential issues.

Use a Flashlight or Sunlight!

- Hold the frame **up to the light**—honey will **glisten**, pollen looks **solid and opaque**, and brood appears **milky or dark depending on age.**

- For **egg detection**, tilt the frame **at an angle with sunlight behind it**

NOTE: Don't be discouraged; most starting beekeepers will loose a hive or two. Urban beekeeping is hard!

Hive Inspection Checklist

Date of Inspection: ___________

Weather Conditions: Temp: ______

Hive Name/Number: ___________

General Hive Condition

[ ] Hive entrance clear of debris

[ ] Bees active at entrance

[ ] No unusual odors (foulbrood, mildew, etc.)

[ ] Hive structure intact (no warping, damage, or leaks)

Bee Behavior

[ ] Calm during inspection

[ ] Bees fanning at entrance (temperature regulation)

[ ] No signs of robbing or excessive aggression

Queen Status

[ ] Queen seen

[ ] Fresh eggs visible

[ ] Good brood pattern (tight, few empty cells)

[ ] Presence of queen cells (note: swarm or supersedure?)

Notes:

____

____

____

Brood Check

[ ] Eggs present

[ ] Larvae present

[ ] Capped brood (worker)

[ ] Capped brood (drone)

[ ] Brood pattern even and solid

Notes:

____

____

🐝 Best Hive Models for Rooftop Beekeeping

1. Langstroth Hive (Most Common & Scalable)

- **Pros:**
  - ✅ Easily expandable with stackable boxes.
  - ✅ Standardized parts & widely available equipment.
  - ✅ Good for maximizing honey production.
- **Cons:**
  - ❌ Heavy to lift (especially full honey boxes).
  - ❌ May need extra insulation against extreme rooftop heat.
- **Best Setup:**
  - Use **medium-sized supers** instead of deep boxes to reduce weight.
  - Place hive on a **stable, level stand** to prevent tipping.
  - Add a **roof cover** or shade cloth to prevent overheating.

2. Warre Hive (Low-Maintenance & Natural Approach)

- **Pros:**
  - ✅ Mimics a hollow tree—bees build their own natural comb.
  - ✅ Less intrusive inspections (good for rooftops with difficult access).
  - ✅ Smaller footprint, making it ideal for compact spaces.
- **Cons:**
  - ❌ Harder to harvest honey compared to Langstroth.
  - ❌ Not as standardized—equipment can be harder to find.
- **Best Setup:**
  - Use **cedar or insulated materials** to protect against rooftop temperature swings.
  - Elevate slightly with a **windbreak** to prevent excessive exposure.

3. Top-Bar Hive (Best for Hobbyists & Gentle Handling)

- **Pros:**
  - ✅ No heavy lifting—honey is harvested from individual bars.
  - ✅ Horizontal design works well for rooftop railings.
  - ✅ Encourages natural beekeeping with minimal intervention.
- **Cons:**
  - ❌ Produces less honey than Langstroth hives.
  - ❌ Requires regular monitoring to prevent cross-comb.

- **Best Setup:**
    - Use a **solid hive stand** to prevent shifting in windy conditions.
    - Ensure **easy access** for hive inspections without excessive bending.

🐝 **Best Hive Models for Backyard Beekeeping**

1. Langstroth Hive (Most Flexible & Easy to Expand)

- **Best for:** Traditional honey production and easy scalability.
- **Setup Tips:**
    - Keep it **facing away from foot traffic** (e.g., against a fence or wall).
    - Add a **fence or tall plants** to encourage bees to fly upward.
    - Consider using **screened bottom boards** for ventilation and pest control.

2. Flow Hive (Easiest Honey Harvesting – Good for Beginners & Small Yards)

- **Pros:**
    - ✅ Allows honey to be harvested without disturbing bees.
    - ✅ Less frequent inspections needed.
    - ✅ Neighbors will love it (no need for a honey extractor).
- **Cons:**
    - ❌ Expensive compared to traditional hives.
    - ❌ Less control over the bees' natural comb building.
- **Best Setup:**
    - Place on **level ground with a hive stand.**
    - Face the entrance toward a **garden or flower bed** to encourage natural foraging.

3. Top-Bar Hive (Great for Small Yards & Gentle Beekeeping)

- **Best for:** Those wanting a natural, low-maintenance beekeeping approach.
- **Setup Tips:**
    - Position under a **tree or shaded area** for temperature regulation.
    - Keep a **small water source** nearby to prevent bees from visiting pools.

Interactive Element: Varroa Mite Monitoring Checklist

Create your own checklist for Varroa mite monitoring in your apiary. Include columns for date, method used (sugar shake or alcohol wash), number of mites counted, and any treatment applied. Regularly updating this checklist will help you identify patterns and make informed decisions about hive management.

Managing Varroa mites requires vigilance and adaptability. You can protect your hives from these pervasive pests by employing integrated pest management strategies, regularly monitoring them, and timing treatments effectively. Through careful observation and proactive measures, you ensure the vitality of your colonies, allowing them to thrive and continue their essential work within our ecosystems.

To determine what's inside a honeycomb, you can use visual inspection, touch, and sometimes even sound. Here's how to tell the difference between honey, pollen, and brood inside a comb

Chapter 3: Seasonal Strategies for Hive Success

Growing up amidst the rhythmic hum of bees, I witnessed firsthand the seasonal dance that defines beekeeping. My formative years were spent observing the subtle yet profound interactions between human care and the natural world. Each year, as the chill of winter approached, my grandfather would meticulously prepare the hives, transforming them into snug sanctuaries against the cold. It was akin to a sacred ritual steeped in care and foresight, ensuring the bees could weather the harsh months ahead. This practice of winterizing hives is not merely about survival; it is an essential preparation that lays the groundwork for future productivity and vitality, setting the stage for a flourishing new year.

Preparing Hives for Winter: Insulation and Feeding

Winter preparation is pivotal in the life cycle of beekeeping. As temperatures plummet, bees cease their foraging activities and retreat into the supportive warmth of the hive, relying heavily on the reserves they have meticulously built up throughout the blossoming months. Without meticulous preparation, colonies are at risk of facing starvation or falling victim to the biting cold. Ensuring that your hives are winter-ready increases their chances of survival and primes them for a vigorous resurgence when the vibrant hues of spring arrive. This intricate process involves insulating the hive to conserve precious warmth and supplementing natural food supplies when they threaten to dwindle dangerously low.

Insulating your hives is essential for minimizing heat loss and thereby protecting your bees from the unyielding harshness of winter conditions. Start by sealing any evident cracks or gaps in the hive structure, as even small openings can allow cold air to penetrate, disrupting the bees' ability to maintain the stable internal temperature critical to their survival. Consider utilizing insulated wraps or foam board installations around the exterior of the hive. These materials are practical barriers against the fierce wind and chilling cold, maintaining a warmer interior world without compromising essential ventilation. Another time-tested technique involves placing straw bales or hay around the perimeter of the hive, which acts as a natural insulative layer, effectively buffering against inevitable temperature fluctuations.

Feeding strategies during the desolate winter months are crucial in supporting your bees when natural resources become woefully scarce. As flowers fade and the nectar-rich landscape recedes into memory, your bees rely solely on the stored honey to sustain themselves. However, supplemental feeding becomes a necessary lifeline if honey reserves run insufficiently. One method is to provide sugar syrup in a feeder positioned above or beside the hive. This sweet mixture mimics the natural nectar, offering an alternative and accessible energy source. Alternatively, fondant or candy boards can be placed directly atop the frames, providing a solid and readily accessible food source that bees can reach without leaving the warmth of the cluster.

Timely winter preparations are the key to ensuring that each task is completed meticulously before severe weather sets in with its full force. Begin insulation efforts in late fall, ideally by mid-November, aligning with your local climate as a reliable guide. This timing allows you to address any structural repairs and apply insulating materials before temperatures drop significantly. As for feeding, assessing honey reserves early in the autumn is wise; start supplementing if needed by late October or early November. This will ensure that your bees have ample time to adjust to new food sources and build up the necessary stores indispensable for their survival before the onset of winter dormancy settles in.

Interactive Element: Winter Preparation Checklist

Create a comprehensive checklist for winterizing your hives. Include essential tasks such as sealing gaps, applying insulation, and preparing feeders. Use this list each year to ensure no essential steps are overlooked. Regularly updating and refining your checklist based on tangible observations and experience will continually hone your approach over time, allowing for greater efficiency and success in future years.

As you prepare your hives for winter, remember that these efforts extend beyond mere survival.

Interactive Element: Winter Preparation Checklist

Create a comprehensive checklist for winterizing your hives. Include essential tasks such as sealing gaps, applying insulation, and preparing feeders. Use this list each year to ensure no essential steps are overlooked. Regularly updating and refining your checklist based on tangible observations and experience will continually hone your approach over time, allowing for greater efficiency and success in future years.

As you prepare your hives for winter, remember that these efforts extend beyond mere survival. They reflect a deep and abiding commitment to nurturing your colonies through the most challenging months, laying a solid foundation for a renewed vigor when warmth inevitably returns to grace the land. Each step in this process strengthens your connection to the natural cycles that govern beekeeping. In doing so, it enhances both your practical skill and appreciation for this rewarding and timeless craft, an endeavor that rewards with both honey and harmony.

Spring Hive Revival: Boosting Activity After Dormancy

As winter relinquishes its icy grip and the first tendrils of warmth begin to unfurl across the vibrant, awakening landscape, your hives stir gently from their long, quiet winter slumber. This moment, the initial spring inspection, is a pivotal transition point for your beekeeping journey, akin to opening a long-sealed door to a world teeming with possibility and the promise of renewal. As you carefully approach your hives, your primary task becomes that of an attentive steward, intent on assessing the overall health and vitality of your colonies. During this pivotal check-up, look for telltale signs of disease or pest infestations that may have insidiously taken hold during the dormant months. The presence of a robust and thriving brood nest is a crucial indicator; it signals the health of your queen, assuring you of a hearty and promising start to the new season. Such a vibrant brood pattern is not just a marker of the colony's current vitality, but a glimpse into the prosperous months that lie ahead. Equally essential in these early inspections is ensuring that the bees have sufficient food reserves remaining, as the capriciousness of early spring weather can still bring about unexpected chills that delay the availability of natural forage in the environment.

To invigorate your bees and jumpstart their activity as temperatures rise, there are several techniques that can be skillfully introduced with careful consideration and patience. Begin by verifying that the hive is adequately ventilated and free from any excess moisture, as a dry and aerated environment encourages movement and productivity among the bees. This sets a welcoming stage for their renewed activity. You might consider providing a light sugar syrup, offering an immediate energy boost that is particularly beneficial if natural nectar sources are still scarce. This artificial nectar serves as both a nutritious lifeline and a stimulus for the bees, encouraging them to start foraging earnestly, thus aligning their efforts with nature's timetable. Additionally, you may strategically place pollen patties inside the hive. These act as an essential supplement, delivering the necessary protein vital for supporting brood rearing. This crucial provision fosters population growth and vigor during this critical phase, aiding the colony in strengthening its numbers after the winter's ebb.

As spring progresses, the bees, invigorated by both natural and supplemental sustenance, become more active. This surge of energy sees them naturally expanding both their numbers and storage spaces within the hive. Managing this expansion efficiently is crucial to avoid overcrowding, a condition that can trigger the urgent, instinctual urge to swarm. Regularly inspecting the hive to monitor brood development and honey storage is prudent; these observations will guide your decision-making in terms of when to add additional supers. Adding supers early, ahead of congestion, provides the bees with room to grow and operate unhindered, maintaining their momentum and continuity. If you begin to notice queen cells forming within the hive, this can be a clear indication of the colony's readiness to swarm. In such scenarios, proactive measures such as hive-splitting or further expanding the available space may be warranted to effectively accommodate this exuberant growth.

The timing of these activities plays a critical role in ensuring that spring tasks are executed with precision and in harmony with the natural rhythms of your bees. Commence inspections once consistent warmer days make their appearance, typically when temperatures reach around 13°C (55°F). Such temperatures allow you to examine the hive without risking the chilling of the delicate brood. Plan to introduce feeding supplements shortly after these inspections if deemed necessary, allowing the bees time to acclimate and fully benefit from the additional nutrition. Adding supers can take place as soon as you observe a notable increase in bee activity, or when nectar flows are anticipated to arrive, often by mid-spring.

The vitality of your hives during springtime not only enables their survival but sets a foundation for a productive and abundant year ahead. Each intentional action you take—be it inspecting, feeding, or expanding—intertwines with the bees' inherent behaviors, fostering a symbiotic relationship that enhances both their survival and your continued success as a beekeeper. The bustling activity within the hive mirrors the awakening landscape outside, each reflecting and supporting the other in a timeless dance that celebrates the renewal of life. This vibrant season symbolizes more than mere survival; it is about thriving in unison, together in harmony with nature's eternal rhythms, laying the groundwork for thriving in the abundant promise of longer, warmer days to come.

Summer Honey Harvesting Techniques

The sun reaches its zenith during summer, casting long, golden rays over your garden. This is when your hives, bustling with energy, brim with honey. Timing your harvest to align with this natural peak is crucial. Typically, the best period to extract honey is just after the main nectar flow has concluded. For many regions, this usually falls between mid-June and early August. Bees cap their honey with a thin layer of wax when it's ready, a telltale sign that it's time to harvest. Harvesting too early can result in honey that's not fully ripened, with higher moisture content that might lead to fermentation. Waiting too long, on the other hand, risks the bees consuming more of their stores or swarming due to overcrowding.

When it comes to harvesting, safety and efficiency are paramount. Start by gently smoking the hive entrance. This calms the bees and reduces stress on the colony. Carefully remove the frames one by one, checking that at least 80% of the honey cells are capped. Use a bee brush to gently sweep any lingering bees back into the hive. This minimizes disturbances and prevents bees from getting trapped in the extraction process. Once you've collected your frames, it's time to uncap the honey. Using a serrated knife or uncapping comb, carefully remove the wax layer to expose the honey beneath. Place the frames in an extractor and spin at a steady speed, allowing centrifugal force to draw out the honey without damaging the comb.

After extraction, your focus shifts to proper storage and processing, ensuring that the quality of your honey remains intact. Pouring honey through a fine mesh strainer helps to remove any stray wax particles or impurities, leaving behind pure, clear liquid gold. Store it in airtight glass jars or food-safe plastic containers to protect it from moisture and contaminants. Honey naturally resists spoilage thanks to its low water content and acidic pH, but storing it in a cool, dry place extends its shelf life and preserves its flavor profiles. If crystallization occurs—a natural process where glucose separates from water—gently warming the jar in a pan of warm water dissolves the crystals without altering the honey's taste or nutritional value.

Once your harvest is complete, returning attention to hive management ensures ongoing colony health and productivity. Post-harvest checks are vital as they reveal insights into the state of your hive after honey removal. Begin by inspecting brood patterns and checking for signs of stress or disease that might have gone unnoticed amid the bustle of summer activity. Verify that your queen is present and laying eggs, as her absence could spell trouble for future colony growth. Assess pollen stores and remaining honey reserves; sufficient resources are essential as summer wanes and autumn approaches.

Consider reapplying treatments for pests like Varroa mites during this period when mite populations tend to spike. Ensuring that these parasites remain under control is crucial for maintaining your bees' health as they prepare for cooler months ahead. If necessary, provide supplemental feeding with sugar syrup to help bolster their reserves while nectar sources dwindle toward season's end.

Reflect on this cycle of care and reward—how nurturing your bees leads not only to bountiful harvests but also strengthens your ties to them and their intricate world. Summer's warmth fades slowly into memory, leaving behind jars of amber sweetness and busy hives readying themselves for what's next.

Each task undertaken throughout this process intertwines with nature's ebb and flow—a continuous dance of giving and receiving between you and your bees. By understanding these rhythms intimately, you cultivate not only honey but also wisdom and respect for this ancient craft that holds nature in balance.

Fall Hive Maintenance: Preparing for the Cold

As autumn leaves transform into a splendid tapestry of gold, amber, and crimson, and the air adopts a distinctive crispness, the rhythm of beekeeping undergoes its cyclical adjustment yet again. The orchestration of fall hive management is a vital chapter in the beekeeper's annual dance, a time when meticulous preparation and unwavering vigilance are required. This seasonal preparation delineates the fine line between a prospering colony that navigates the winter with aplomb and a colony that flounders amidst the chill. As temperatures begin to plummet, bees face the formidable challenge of preserving their crucial warmth, as well as accessing an adequate supply of nourishing food. Within this period, your duty is that of a conscientious custodian, ensuring your hives are singularly well-prepared to weather the forthcoming frigid months.

Attentive Fall Inspections

During your fall inspections, the emphasis should be placed primarily on accurately assessing the hive's strength and overall health, which requires a discerning eye and a methodical approach. Initiate the process by scrupulously checking for any discernible signs of disease or burgeoning pest infestations, with particular vigilance for Varroa mites. These nefarious parasites often proliferate as the summer heat gives way to cooler days. A robust colony is signaled by healthy brood patterns, and the strong presence of a queen is a positive indicator, displaying the colony's readiness to endure winter. Delve further into examining honey stores meticulously, as bees' survival hinges on the adequacy of their reserves during months when foraging is wholly unfeasible. Should these stores present as insufficient, immediate remedial steps must be considered to enhance them. Furthermore, the hive's physical condition merits careful attention. Conduct a thorough inspection to confirm the structural integrity of each hive. Ensuring that the boxes fit snugly together with no gaps or vulnerabilities that might permit cold air or moisture to intrude is vital for the bees' protection.

Strategic Fall Feeding

Feeding strategies in the fall are paramount to reinforcing your bees' winter reserves. With the natural decline of nectar sources, your bees will likely necessitate supplementary feeding to fortify their sustenance. It's advisable to employ a more viscous sugar syrup compared to the spring formula—a 2:1 sugar-to-water ratio is ideal, providing concentrated energy. Offer this syrup as early in autumn as conceivable, granting ample time for your industrious bees to process and adeptly store it before the ambient temperatures fall too drastically. The strategic goal remains ensuring your bees enter winter with full reserves tucked away in their honeycombs, ready for the long months ahead.

Timeliness and Thoughtful Execution

Timing holds the essence in fall preparations, and accurate execution enhances its efficacy. Commence your inspections early in the season, preferentially by late September, when temperatures remain accommodation for hive inspections without inducing undue distress upon your bees. Beginning feeding promptly, particularly once inspections imply insufficient reserves, is typically advisable by early October. Allowing several weeks for your bees to prepare the vital reserves before the cold snap ultimately descends.

Ensuring a Prosperous Future for Your Bees

The profound significance of meticulous fall preparation cannot be overstated. By decisively ensuring that your hives are both healthy and well-provisioned at this juncture, you effectively lay the foundation for their survival during the harsh embrace of winter. Every task executed during this time serves as an investment into the future vitality and productivity of your colonies when spring's blossoms make their awaited return.

Reflecting on Cyclical Seasonal Strategies

As this chapter reaches its denouement, it is crucial to reflect on how every seasonal strategy builds seamlessly upon its predecessor, forging a continuous cycle of care and keen observation. Your dedicated efforts throughout these seasons craft an unbroken chain that intricately connects you to your bees and the natural world in which they thrive. These laborious yet indispensable efforts not only underpin their survival but also enrich your understanding of the sublime natural rhythms that shepherd us all, crafting a tapestry of interconnectedness.

Anticipating the forthcoming chapter, Chapter 4 will delve deeply into the pivotal role bees play in bolstering garden ecosystems, enhancing biodiversity, and fostering plant life beyond the tangible confines of their hives. Gaining insight into this interconnectedness serves not merely to deepen appreciation but also kindles inspiration to nurture our gardens and bees with informed intention and tender care.

Chapter 4: The Role of Bees in Garden Ecosystems

Pollination Power: How Bees Boost Your Garden

Imagine stepping into a radiant garden where every flower unfurls with vivid hues, the air is imbued with a harmonious symphony of soft buzzing, and the atmosphere is alive with a tangible energy. This enchanting scene could be your reality, owing to the relentless endeavors of bees. These diligent and tireless insects are pivotal players in the art of pollination, a complex and vital biological process that is at the heart of plant reproduction. As bees busily forage for nectar, they inadvertently become agents of pollination, transferring pollen from the male anthers of one flower to the female stigma of another. This seemingly straightforward act lays the groundwork for plant reproduction, allowing flowers to set seeds and produce fruit—a miraculous transformation from bloom to bounty.

The significance of pollination reaches far beyond the scope of a single plant. It is absolutely essential for maintaining garden biodiversity—a rich tapestry intricately woven with a diverse array of species that coexist and flourish together. Bees are paramount in this endeavor, as they traverse various flowers, ensuring genetic diversity and robust growth. This diversity acts as a formidable shield, building resilience and allowing your garden to withstand an array of challenges including pesky intruders, diseases, and shifts in weather patterns. With each dedicated visit, bees uphold a complex web of life, nurturing everything from resplendent blooms to the myriad creatures that are dependent on them.

The benefits that stem from bee pollination are particularly palpable when considering crop yields and their intrinsic quality. Numerous fruits and vegetables are reliant on bees to reach their pinnacle of production. Research has highlighted that bee-pollinated crops typically yield more abundant harvests with larger and more flavorful fruits. For example, strawberries that benefit from bee pollination can be not only juicier but also exhibit a more uniform shape compared to those pollinated by alternative methods. This enhanced quality elevates your culinary creations and also plays a pivotal role in contributing to a more sustainable and dependable food system. By supporting and fostering pollinators, you invest in this crucial and interwoven chain.

Beyond the immediate and tangible advantages of bolstered yields and enriched flavor, bees also play a key role in maintaining ecological balance within your garden ecosystem. They act as keystone species, entities whose presence significantly influences the survival and prosperity of numerous other organisms. By facilitating pollination, bees promote the growth of plants that offer both habitat and sustenance for a wide variety of creatures, from diminutive insects to vibrant birds. This intertwined network nurtures harmony and equilibrium, reducing the likelihood of ecological imbalances and fostering a thriving and sustainable environment.

The role of bees in gardens transcends their immediate influence on plants and crops. Their presence offers invaluable educational opportunities for individuals spanning all ages. Observing bees as they diligently perform their tasks provides profound insights into their complex social structures and unrelenting work ethic. This connection to nature ignites curiosity, inspiring a profound appreciation for the delicate balance inherent in ecosystems. As you watch bees expertly navigate from bloom to bloom, you witness nature's intricate choreography—a timeless dance that has unfolded over millennia and continues to shape our world in myriad and marvelous ways.

Interactive Element: Observing Pollination

Devote meaningful time in your garden meticulously observing the activity of these industrious bees. Pay careful attention to the specific flowers they tend to visit most frequently and take note of how they skillfully move between blooms. Consider maintaining a detailed journal to document your observations over an extended period. Reflect on how these interactions critically contribute to the overarching health and diversity of your garden ecosystem, and the broader tapestry of life it supports.

The presence of bees in your garden represents not just a privilege but a profound responsibility. By thoughtfully creating and maintaining an environment that bolsters their essential work, you contribute to a larger, broader effort to protect these indispensable pollinators and ensure the sustained health and resilience of our planet's ecosystems. Each moment spent fostering this environment is a step toward safeguarding a future brimming with life, diversity, and the ongoing potential for growth and renewal.

Integrating Bees with Existing Garden Layouts

Introducing bees into an already flourishing garden can be a seamless and rewarding process when approached with thoughtful planning and creativity. The first step is to assess your current garden layout, identifying areas that can naturally accommodate hives without disrupting the existing harmony. Look for sunny spots sheltered from strong winds, as bees thrive in warmth and calm environments. Acknowledge the flight paths of your future bees; they prefer unobstructed routes to and from their hive. Consider placing hives near existing shrubs or tall plants that can act as natural windbreaks, ensuring bees have a tranquil space to land and take off.

Designing a bee-friendly space doesn't require a complete garden overhaul. Instead, focus on incorporating elements that naturally encourage bee activity and integration. Start by enhancing diversity within your flower beds. Integrate a variety of flowering plants that bloom throughout different seasons, ensuring a constant supply of nectar and pollen. Encourage layers in your planting, using a mix of heights and textures to create an inviting habitat. Consider adding features like small water sources—bees need hydration too. A simple shallow dish with stones or floating corks allows bees to safely land and drink without drowning.

One common concern when introducing bees is the potential for increased bee traffic in areas frequented by family or visitors. Address this by creatively designing pathways that gently guide foot traffic away from hive entrances, using natural barriers or visual cues like low fences or hedges. If space allows, create dedicated zones for bees, subtly separated from high-traffic areas. Educate visitors about bee behavior and the importance of maintaining respectful distances from hives. This awareness fosters coexistence and appreciation rather than trepidation.

Another challenge is ensuring that introducing bees doesn't upset the balance of your garden's ecosystem. Monitor the interplay between your existing flora and the new pollinators. Bees are generally harmonious partners in any garden, but it's wise to observe how their presence might affect other pollinators or wildlife. Should competition for resources arise, consider augmenting your garden with additional flowering plants or adjusting watering schedules to support all inhabitants. Regular observation and adaptability are key to maintaining equilibrium.

Case studies offer valuable insights into successful bee integration within diverse garden settings. For instance, a small urban garden in New York City transformed its space by introducing bees alongside an array of native plants. The gardeners strategically placed hives against a south-facing wall, maximizing sunlight exposure while minimizing wind interference. They planted a mixture of perennial flowers and herbs like lavender and thyme, which thrived in the urban microclimate and provided sustenance for the bees year-round. As a result, the garden not only flourished but also became a local sanctuary for various pollinators, teaching neighbors about urban biodiversity.

In another example, a suburban family garden faced initial challenges with bee placement due to limited space and neighbor concerns. By collaborating with neighboring gardeners, they expanded their pollinator-friendly habitat beyond individual property lines, creating a cohesive neighborhood environment rich in resources for bees. This collective effort not only mitigated individual challenges but also fostered community bonds and shared stewardship of local biodiversity.

These examples illustrate that integrating bees into an existing garden layout is both achievable and beneficial when approached with creativity, mindfulness, and collaboration. The introduction of these industrious insects not only enhances the vibrancy of your garden but also deepens your connection to the natural world around you. By embracing bee-friendly practices and fostering environments that support pollinators, you contribute to a healthier ecosystem that thrives in harmony with human presence.

As you embark on this endeavor, remember that each garden is unique, offering its own set of opportunities and challenges. Your role as a steward involves continual learning and adaptation, allowing you to nurture both your garden and its newest inhabitants with care and understanding.

Creating Bee-Friendly Plantings

Designing your garden with bees in mind invites a vibrant dance of life into your outdoor space. To attract and support these vital pollinators year-round, it's crucial to plant species that offer an abundant supply of nectar and pollen. Lavender, with its fragrant purple blooms, is a perennial favorite among bees, providing nourishment from early spring through late summer. Sunflowers, towering and radiant, offer both food and habitat, drawing bees with their bright, open faces. For an early spring feast, plant crocuses and snowdrops that burst forth with color and sustenance just as bees awaken from their winter rest. In the autumn, asters and goldenrods provide crucial late-season resources, ensuring bees have the sustenance they need to prepare for winter.

The importance of plant diversity cannot be overstated when considering bee health. A diverse selection of plants not only attracts a wider range of bee species but also ensures that nectar and pollen are available throughout the seasons. This diversity mirrors the natural habitats bees thrive in, providing a rich tapestry of colors, shapes, and textures that cater to varied bee preferences and needs. Such variety ensures that even the pickiest pollinators find something to dine on, strengthening their populations. Additionally, diverse plantings help buffer against disease and pest outbreaks, as a wider range of plants can support beneficial insects that naturally manage garden pests.

Arranging your plants thoughtfully enhances their attractiveness to bees. Grouping similar plants together creates a more noticeable target for bees. They can easily move from flower to flower without expending unnecessary energy searching for isolated blooms. This clustering mimics natural floral displays, making it easier for bees to gather resources efficiently. Consider planting in drifts or clusters rather than isolated patches; this not only improves visual appeal but also maximizes the garden's allure to bees. Height variation in planting can also be beneficial. Taller plants like hollyhocks can serve as beacons, guiding bees to lower-growing favorites like clover or hyssop nestled below.

Companion planting adds another layer of depth to bee-friendly gardens. Some plants naturally enhance each other's growth and health when planted in close proximity. For instance, borage is known not only for its star-shaped blue flowers that bees adore but also for its ability to improve the flavor of nearby strawberries. Marigolds, often used as companion plants for vegetables like tomatoes or peppers, repel harmful pests while attracting beneficial insects, including bees. These symbiotic relationships create a dynamic ecosystem where plants and pollinators thrive together. Incorporating a variety of companion plants not only boosts bee visitation but also promotes overall garden health by enhancing soil quality and reducing pest pressures.

When planning your garden, consider the needs of different bee species. While honeybees are generalists, many native bees have specific plant preferences or requirements. Mason bees, for example, are particularly drawn to fruit blossoms like apple or cherry trees. Meanwhile, bumblebees favor tubular flowers such as foxgloves or penstemons that accommodate their larger bodies. By including a mix of plant types that cater to these different preferences, you cultivate a garden that's not only buzzing with activity but also supports a wide range of pollinators.

Creating a bee-friendly garden is about more than just planting flowers; it's about fostering an environment where bees feel welcome and safe. Avoiding pesticides and opting for organic gardening practices ensures that your garden remains a healthy haven for pollinators. Providing habitat features like bee hotels or leaving some areas of bare soil caters to ground-nesting bees who might otherwise struggle to find suitable nesting sites in manicured spaces. Water sources are another consideration; a shallow dish with rocks can provide bees with a safe place to drink, helping them stay hydrated during hot summer days.

As you cultivate your garden with these considerations in mind, you'll notice an increase in bee activity and diversity. This not only enhances the vitality of your garden but also contributes to broader ecological health by supporting these crucial pollinators. Each plant you choose, each arrangement you create, plays a part in this dynamic ecosystem, ensuring that your garden remains a vibrant and flourishing sanctuary for both bees and humans alike.

Understanding Nectar Flow and Its Impact on Productivity

Unseen yet pivotal, nectar flow is the lifeblood that fuels your hive's vitality, driving both productivity and bee behavior. At its core, nectar flow refers to the availability of nectar in flowering plants, a critical resource that fluctuates with seasonal changes and environmental conditions. This flow dictates how bees forage, influencing the dynamics within the hive. When nectar is abundant, bees work tirelessly, collecting and converting it into honey. This abundance not only sustains the colony but also enhances hive productivity, allowing bees to thrive and store reserves for leaner times.

Tracking nectar flow in your garden requires keen observation and knowledge of local flowering patterns. Note the bloom times of your plants and monitor them closely. Keep an eye on weather conditions; rain can wash away nectar, while extreme heat might dry it up. By understanding these patterns, you can time your interventions to optimize nectar availability. You might choose to plant a variety of flowers that bloom at different times, ensuring a continuous nectar supply. Additionally, supplementing with artificial nectar sources during periods of scarcity can help maintain hive productivity.

Nectar flow directly influences bee behavior, shaping how they interact with their environment and each other. During periods of high nectar flow, bees exhibit increased foraging activity, often traveling greater distances and visiting more flowers. This heightened activity can lead to increased hive congestion as bees return with their bounty. Inside the hive, you'll notice a bustling atmosphere with bees busy storing and processing nectar. Conversely, when nectar is scarce, bees may become more defensive, guarding their limited resources more fiercely. Understanding these behavioral shifts allows you to manage your hive more effectively, ensuring harmony and productivity.

Successful nectar flow management involves a combination of observation, intervention, and adaptation. Consider the example of a small apiary situated in a suburban garden, where the beekeeper noticed a lull in bee activity during midsummer. By planting late-blooming perennials like sedum and asters, they extended the nectar season, revitalizing bee foraging and boosting honey production. Another case involved an urban rooftop garden where limited space posed a challenge for continuous flowering. The gardener strategically placed planters with diverse, nectar-rich plants such as borage and salvia, creating a vibrant oasis that attracted pollinators even in an urban setting.

These examples underscore the importance of understanding and managing nectar flow to sustain bee activity and hive health. By creating a thriving environment that aligns with natural rhythms, you not only enhance your bees' productivity but also contribute to broader ecological health. This approach fosters resilience against environmental fluctuations, ensuring that your garden remains a haven for pollinators year-round.

As we conclude this chapter on the crucial role of bees in garden ecosystems, it's essential to reflect on how these small creatures play an outsized role in our world. Their tireless work supports biodiversity, enhances crop yields, and maintains ecological balance—all while enriching our gardens with life and color. Looking ahead to our next chapter, we will explore advanced hive management strategies that further optimize your beekeeping endeavors. By building on the foundation laid here, you'll continue to nurture thriving colonies that not only benefit your garden but also contribute to the health of our planet's ecosystems.

Chapter 5: Advanced Hive Management Techniques

Decoding Swarming: Prevention and Control

On a sweltering afternoon, drenched in the golden hue of the summer sun, I stood beside my grandfather, a seasoned beekeeper whose hands had nurtured generations of bees. Together, we watched in rapt attention as bees poured out of their hive like a living, buzzing river. It was my first encounter with swarming, an awe-inspiring yet bewildering spectacle, a scene that seemed tailor-made for an ancient fable of natural continuity. Swarming is an intrinsic part of bee life, a natural expansion mechanism that ensures both genetic diversity and the long-term survival of the colony. In essence, swarming is the bees' way of propagating the species in the grand tapestry of life. When a hive becomes crowded or the queen's pheromones, the chemical signals she emits, start to lose potency, the hive instinctively prepares to swarm by raising new queens. In this remarkable display of natural organization, the old queen departs, taking a portion of the colony with her, in search of a new home. This exodus leaves behind an orderly succession of a new leader, ensuring the hive continues to flourish.

Spotting the signs of an impending swarm demands a keen eye and a deep familiarity with bee behavior, almost like learning the nuances of a subtle language. Early indicators tend to reveal themselves through increased hive activity—an unusual hustle and bustle—as well as the construction of numerous queen cells. These elongated structures, often likened to tiny peanuts due to their peculiar appearance, hang prominently from the frames as harbingers of change. Moreover, you might notice a clustering of bees at the hive entrance, or detect unusual traffic patterns, signaling the bees' preparation for a collective departure. Observing these subtle yet significant cues allows you to anticipate and mitigate swarming before it wreaks havoc across your apiary.

To curb swarming tendencies, proactive hive management emerges as a necessity, not just a strategy. One effective method is ensuring there is ample space within the hive for the bees to expand. Regularly adding supers during nectar flows—when flowers are bountiful and bees most industrious—helps alleviate congestion and significantly reduces the urge to swarm. Additionally, rotating frames and removing old combs are crucial practices that maintain a fresh, vibrant environment, thereby discouraging overcrowding and its undesirable consequences. Hive inspections are particularly important in spring when swarming impulses peak like the renewed energy of the season itself. During these checks, removing queen cells can deter swarming, though this approach is not infallible and requires vigilant follow-up. Alternatively, dividing a robust colony into two smaller ones provides additional living space, fulfilling the bees' innate drive for expansion without the need for drastic relocation.

Yet, despite even the most diligent efforts, swarms sometimes escape, leaving a visible gap in your once-packed apiary. When this occurs, capturing the swarm becomes paramount, both to preserve your investment and to maintain hive numbers for future harvests. Approach the swarm calmly and with reverence; bees are often docile during this transitory phase. Equip yourself with a large cardboard box or an empty hive body to collect them without harm. Gently shake or brush the cluster into your container, ensuring you capture the queen, whose presence is pivotal to the swarm's cohesion and eventual settlement. Once secured, transfer the swarm to a prepared hive with empty frames and foundation, a new canvas awaiting their industrious touch. Providing a sugar syrup feeder will encourage them to quickly make themselves at home in their new abode, spanning fresh combs with the vigor of newly begun chapters.

Interactive Element: Swarm Management Checklist

Create a comprehensive checklist for managing swarms effectively, designed to serve both novice and seasoned beekeepers alike. This must include detailed steps for identifying early signs of swarming, along with practical preventive measures that align with natural bee instincts. Additionally, detail safe swarm capture techniques that prioritize the well-being of the bees, ensuring their smooth transition back into managed hives. This tool will serve as an indispensable, practical guide during the bustling peak swarming seasons when hive defensive lines are most vulnerable.

Swarming, though challenging in its execution, is a testament to the vitality and resilience of your bees—a natural phenomenon that encapsulates the essence of continuity and renewal. By delving into its triggers with a learned eye and implementing strategic interventions, you can adeptly manage this indispensable process while enjoying the immense satisfaction of maintaining a thriving, harmonious apiary. Let this journey into the world of swarming enrich your appreciation and understanding of these remarkable creatures whose lives intertwine so closely with our own.

Queen Rearing and Replacement: Best Practices

In the intricate hierarchy of a bee colony, the queen reigns supreme, her presence influencing every aspect of hive life. The queen's vitality and genetic traits profoundly impact colony health, productivity, and temperament. A robust queen lays up to 2,000 eggs daily, ensuring a steady flow of workers to forage, care for brood, and defend the hive. Her pheromones, the chemical signals she emits, maintain harmony, suppressing worker bees' reproductive instincts while galvanizing them into action. When the queen falters due to age or illness, productivity wanes, and hive cohesion falters, leading to unrest or loss.

Raising your own queens within the apiary offers control over genetic traits, allowing you to select for qualities such as disease resistance and gentleness. One popular method is grafting, where larvae are transferred into artificial queen cups. This technique requires precision but yields excellent results. Another approach is the use of the Cloake board method, which involves manipulating hive conditions to encourage queen rearing naturally. Both methods demand close monitoring to ensure larval development proceeds smoothly, with the ultimate goal of nurturing strong, viable queens ready to lead.

The process of selecting and introducing replacement queens is both art and science. Begin by choosing queens from hives exhibiting desirable traits—high honey production, low aggression, and disease resilience. Once selected, introduce the new queen with care to ensure acceptance. Place her in a cage within the hive for several days, allowing workers to acclimate to her scent gradually. This period reduces the risk of rejection or aggression upon release. Monitor closely after release for signs of acceptance, such as bees tending to her rather than displaying hostility.

Timing plays a crucial role in successful queen rearing. Optimal conditions for queen development include warm temperatures and abundant forage. Spring and early summer are ideal periods when nectar flows are strong, providing ample resources for new colonies. Avoid rearing queens during adverse weather or dearth periods when resources are scarce. Environmental factors also influence queen quality. Ensure hives receive adequate sunlight and protection from harsh winds, as these elements affect brood incubation and overall hive activity.

A case study of a small-scale beekeeper illustrates these principles in action. In the early spring, noticing a decline in honey yield and increased hive agitation, the beekeeper decided to replace aging queens across several hives. Using grafting techniques honed over years of practice, they carefully selected larvae from high-performing colonies known for gentle temperament and disease resistance. The new queens were introduced during a period of abundant bloom, ensuring ample resources for colony expansion. Over successive weeks, the beekeeper monitored hives meticulously, noting improved brood patterns and increased worker activity.

This experience underscores the profound impact of queen quality on hive dynamics. A well-chosen queen not only invigorates her colony but also enhances the entire apiary's performance. By mastering queen rearing and replacement techniques, beekeepers gain autonomy over their operations, fostering resilient hives capable of thriving in diverse conditions.

The knowledge gained from these practices extends beyond individual colonies, contributing to broader efforts in bee conservation and sustainability. Through careful selection and breeding, beekeepers play a vital role in preserving genetic diversity within bee populations. This diversity acts as a bulwark against emerging threats such as pests and climate change, ensuring that future generations inherit healthy, vibrant bee communities.

In your beekeeping journey, remember that patience and observation are key allies in nurturing queens. Each step in the process offers an opportunity to deepen your understanding of bee behavior and biology. As you implement these techniques within your apiary, you'll witness firsthand the transformative power of a thriving queen—a testament to nature's resilience and your role as a steward of its wonders.

Expanding Your Apiary: Adding New Hives

The thought of expanding your apiary carries with it a blend of excitement and responsibility. Before setting up additional hives, evaluate several key factors to determine whether expansion is feasible and beneficial. Consider the current health and productivity of your existing colonies. Strong, thriving hives are more likely to support successful expansion. Assess the availability of forage in your area, as an increase in bee numbers necessitates ample floral resources to sustain them. Also, review your own capacity, both in terms of time and resources. Adequate time for hive management and financial investment in equipment are crucial for a smooth transition from a small to a larger apiary operation.

Once you've determined that conditions are favorable, hive splitting emerges as a primary method for expanding your bee population. This process involves dividing a strong colony into two separate hives, each with its own queen. Begin by selecting a robust hive with a healthy queen and ample resources. Carefully locate frames filled with brood and stores, as well as some frames containing eggs or young larvae. It's essential to maintain a balance of resources between the original and new hives to ensure both thrive independently. Transfer these frames into a new hive body, ensuring an even distribution of workers between the two colonies. Introducing a new queen to the split hive can speed up its establishment, although allowing it to raise its own queen from young larvae is also viable.

As you integrate new hives into your existing apiary, consider strategies that promote harmony and minimize disruptions. Position new hives with adequate spacing from established ones to reduce competition for resources and prevent drifting, where bees mistakenly enter neighboring hives. This spacing also aids in maintaining distinct hive scents, which are crucial for bees to identify their home. Monitor the behavior of the bees closely during this period. Watch for signs of aggression or robbing, where bees attempt to steal honey from other hives. If such issues arise, adjusting hive placement or adding entrance reducers can help mitigate conflicts and promote peace within the apiary.

However, expanding an apiary isn't merely about biological or logistical considerations; legal aspects must also be factored into your plans. Before adding new hives, familiarize yourself with local regulations regarding beekeeping. Many regions have specific rules about the number of hives allowed per property, as well as guidelines for hive placement concerning property lines and public spaces. Some areas might require registration of your hives or adherence to particular health and safety standards designed to protect both bees and humans. Contact local beekeeping associations or agricultural departments for guidance on compliance with these regulations.

Logistical considerations play an equally significant role in planning your expansion. Evaluate access to the apiary site for routine maintenance and honey harvesting activities. Ensure that there is sufficient space not only for the hives themselves but also for equipment storage and work areas. Accessibility is especially important if you'll need to transport heavy equipment or honey supers regularly. Additionally, consider potential challenges posed by seasonal changes, such as muddy paths or overgrown vegetation, which could hinder access to your hives at certain times of the year.

In practical terms, expanding your apiary involves acquiring additional equipment such as hive bodies, frames, and protective gear. Budget accordingly for these expenses and seek reliable suppliers who can provide quality materials. Investing in durable equipment pays off in the long run by reducing maintenance needs and ensuring the safety of both you and your bees during hive inspections and other activities.

Reflecting on these aspects of apiary expansion draws attention not only to the technicalities involved but also to the broader impact of such growth on your relationship with beekeeping itself. As you increase your hive numbers, you'll likely find yourself more deeply immersed in the rhythms and demands of this ancient practice, gaining insights into bee behavior and ecology that enrich your understanding and appreciation of both the bees themselves and the intricacies of nature's interconnected systems.

This expansion process also invites opportunities for community engagement through educational outreach or collaborative projects with fellow beekeepers or gardeners interested in supporting pollinator populations. Sharing knowledge gained from firsthand experience with others fosters a sense of shared purpose rooted in sustainability—an endeavor that benefits not only individual colonies but entire ecosystems.

The journey toward expanding your apiary encompasses more than just increased honey production; it represents an ongoing commitment to fostering healthy bee populations while simultaneously enhancing biodiversity within your local environment. Each choice made along this path contributes not only to successful hive growth but also strengthens connections between humans and these remarkable pollinators whose diligent work underpins much of our natural world's productivity and resilience.

By thoughtfully navigating each step involved—from evaluating readiness through managing logistics—you lay groundwork for sustainable growth that balances personal goals with broader ecological responsibilities inherent within this rewarding pursuit known as beekeeping.

If you can only have one or two hives due to space or local regulations but find yourself needing more (for example, due to a strong colony, swarming, or expansion), here are some strategies to manage the situation:

🐝 1. Preventing Swarming Instead of Adding Hives

If your colony is growing rapidly and you're worried about overcrowding, you can **prevent swarming** rather than adding new hives.

How to manage an expanding colony:

- ✅ **Add more supers** to give them space for honey storage.

- ✅ **Perform a split but donate or sell the new colony** (see below).

- ✅ **Regularly inspect and remove swarm cells** to discourage swarming.

- ✅ **Use a queen excluder** to manage where she lays eggs.

🐝 2. Splitting Hives Without Adding More to Your Property

If your hive is too strong and you need to split it, but you're at your hive limit, you have a few options:

✅ Give the New Hive Away or Sell It

- Find a local beekeeper who wants a colony.
- Post on local beekeeping groups or clubs to sell/gift a split.

✅ Relocate to a Friend or Shared Space

- Some urban areas have **community gardens or apiaries** where you can place a hive.
- Ask **friends or family with space** if they'd like a hive on their property.

✅ Join a Beekeeping Co-op

- Some beekeeping clubs allow members to keep additional hives in their apiaries.

🐝 3. Using a Nucleus Colony Instead of a Full Hive

If you want to keep extra bees but can't legally have another full hive, consider maintaining a **nucleus colony (nuc)** instead.

- A **nuc is a small 5-frame hive** that can store a backup queen or extra bees.
- If a full hive **dies or struggles**, you can use the nuc to replenish it.
- Some cities don't count nucs toward hive limits—check your local laws.

🐝 4. Working with Other Beekeepers

- Some beekeepers will **host hives on their property** for you in exchange for honey or a share of the hive.
- You could **partner with a local farm or garden** that supports pollinators.

🐝 5. Expanding by Requeening Instead of Adding Hives

If your goal is to **increase honey production rather than bee numbers**, consider **requeening** with a high-producing queen strain instead of adding more colonies

Troubleshooting Common Hive Issues

Beekeeping, while rewarding, presents its share of challenges. Recognizing the symptoms of hive issues early can make a significant difference in maintaining a healthy colony. Bees communicate their distress in subtle ways, and keen observation is your best tool. Look for erratic flight patterns or bees that seem lethargic, indicating potential health problems. Piles of dead bees near the hive entrance may signal pesticide exposure or disease. Additionally, if you notice a lack of brood or spotty brood patterns, these could point to queen issues or disease. Honey stores that appear depleted despite abundant forage suggest robbing by other bees or pests.

Once symptoms are identified, diagnosing the root cause requires a methodical approach. Begin by inspecting the hive thoroughly. Open each frame and look for visible signs of disease, such as discolored larvae or unusual odors. A sour smell can indicate foulbrood, a serious bacterial disease. If pests are suspected, examine the frames and hive body for evidence of Varroa mites or wax moths. Mite populations can be assessed using a sugar roll test; this involves collecting bees and covering them in powdered sugar to dislodge mites for counting. Accurate diagnosis is essential for effective treatment, so take notes and compare them against known symptoms.

Addressing conflicts between hives often involves understanding their root causes. Competition for resources can lead to robbing, where stronger hives target weaker ones. To mitigate this, ensure each hive has adequate food stores and consider installing entrance reducers to limit access. Aggression between hives may be due to drifting, where bees enter neighboring hives by mistake. Maintaining distinct hive scents helps prevent this; placing hives with entrances facing different directions can reduce confusion. Regular inspections help identify issues early, allowing you to take corrective action before conflicts escalate.

For long-term hive health, consider strategies that enhance resilience and sustainability. Strong colonies are less susceptible to disease and pests, so focus on maintaining robust bee populations through proactive management. Rotate old frames with fresh ones to prevent disease buildup and encourage healthy comb development. Regularly assess your queen's performance, replacing her if productivity declines. Diverse forage options support bee nutrition; planting a variety of flowering plants ensures a steady food supply throughout the seasons. Implement integrated pest management practices to minimize chemical use while effectively controlling pests.

These advanced tips can be implemented with relative ease, yet they offer profound benefits for your apiary's well-being. For example, practicing good apiary hygiene by cleaning tools and equipment reduces disease transmission. Providing supplementary feeding during dearth periods supports colony strength when natural resources are scarce. Educating yourself about local bee diseases and pests keeps you prepared to address new challenges as they arise.

A case study exemplifies these principles in action: In a small rural apiary facing persistent Varroa mite issues, the beekeeper implemented a comprehensive pest management plan. They combined mechanical methods like drone brood trapping with organic treatments such as formic acid applications. By monitoring mite levels consistently and adjusting strategies based on results, they successfully reduced mite loads while maintaining strong colonies. This proactive approach not only improved hive health but also increased honey yields over time.

In summary, troubleshooting hive issues requires vigilance, knowledge, and adaptability. By identifying symptoms early and diagnosing root causes accurately, you can address problems before they spiral out of control. Implementing strategies for conflict resolution and long-term health ensures your colonies remain productive and vibrant contributors to local ecosystems.

As you reflect on these techniques, remember that beekeeping is an evolving practice shaped by observation and experience. Each challenge met and overcome enriches your understanding of bee behavior and ecology—knowledge that will serve you well as you explore new horizons in the next chapter dedicated to enhancing honey production and quality through advanced techniques.

WHAT TO DO WHEN

You Have Queen Cells In Your Hive

CHOOSE YOUR OWN ADVENTURE CHART

from Beekeeping Made Simple

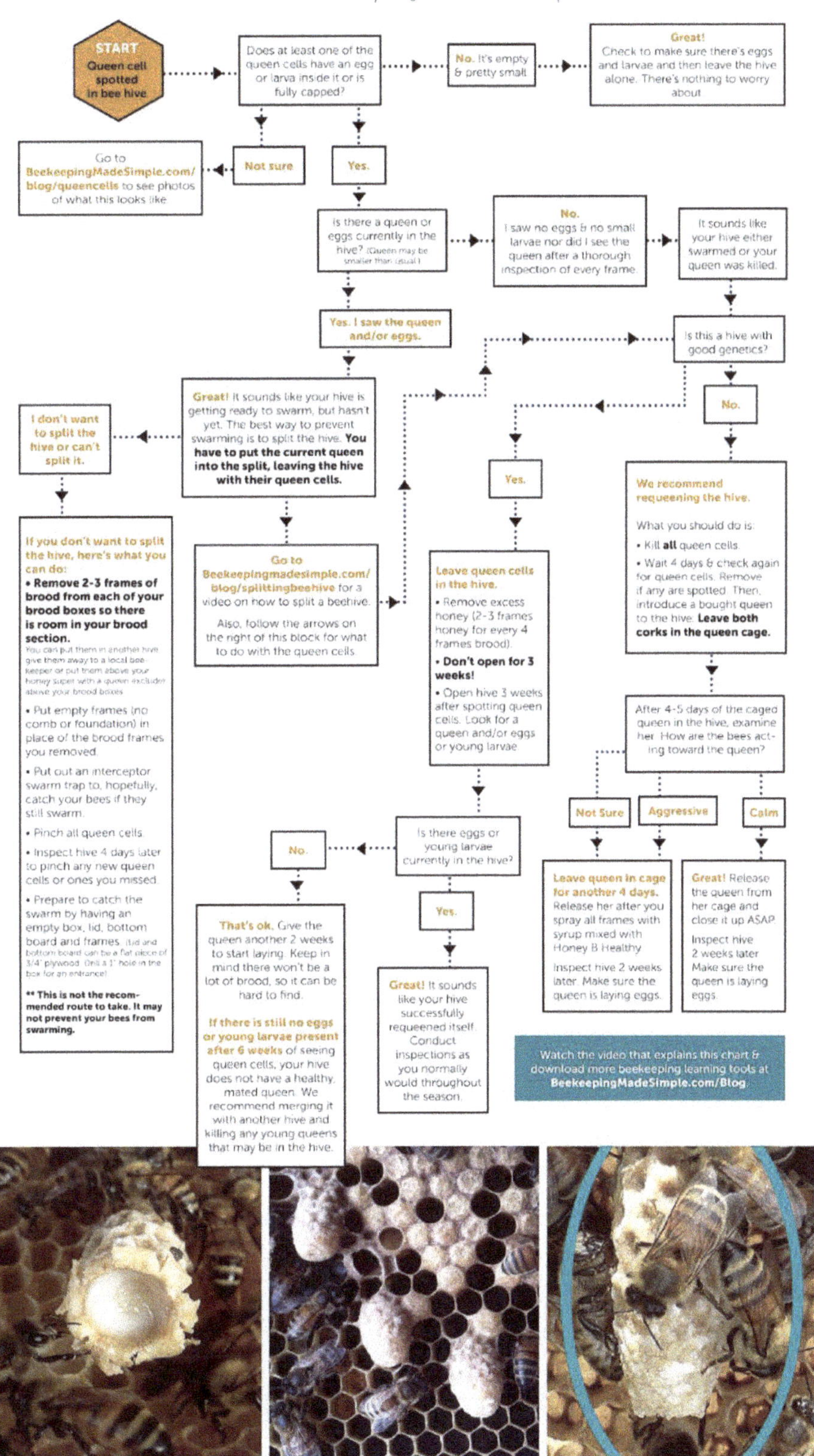

Chapter 6: Safety and Legal Considerations in Beekeeping

— ✱ —

Bee Handling and Sting Prevention Techniques

Reflecting on my initial experience in front of an active hive, the juxtaposition of thrill with apprehension still feels vivid. Standing there, with the rhythm of the bees humming around me, my heart mirrored their tempo in its rapid beat. It was my grandfather's gentle guidance that anchored me, reminding me of the symbiosis between calmness and bees. He imparted the wisdom of understanding that bees possess a sensitivity to the vibrations and energies that humans carry. This profound receptiveness means that any unsettledness or nervous energy can be swiftly picked up by the colony. Thus, grounding oneself in tranquility doesn't merely serve to reduce the possibility of stings; it establishes a rapport based on mutual respect and understanding. Stepping towards a hive with assured calmness provides a silent assurance to the bees that their home remains untouched by threat. This state of mind transforms hive work into an almost meditative practice, one where confidence encourages efficiency and reduces colony disruption.

When it comes to protective gear, it's crucial to consider more than simply suiting up. Just as a knight carefully selects armor best suited to both the battlefield and comfort, a beekeeper should scrutinize their gear with the same care and attention. Protective suits crafted from quality materials promise not just shielding from stings but also the comfort to crouch and lift without restriction. A snugly fitted bee suit operates much like a second skin, barricading any entry points for stings, while also allowing the fluidity needed for all tasks in beekeeping. Veils play an indispensable role, safeguarding those most vulnerable areas—the face and neck—from unforeseen encounters. According to the Betterbee guide, ensuring both durability and comfort through material choice for veils and suits is paramount, an investment into both safety and seamless movement. Gloves, often a topic of debate among seasoned beekeepers, still serve as a reassuring shield for those cultivating familiarity with hive handling.

The art of hive inspection is finely honed through methodology. Your initial act of gently puffing smoke at the hive's entrance functions akin to a 'knock on the door,' signaling your presence in a non-threatening manner. The smoke acts by interrupting their chemical communication, inducing a temporary lull. Move through your inspection with deliberate and controlled motions; bees are creatures of steady habit, and sudden movements can unsettle the hive's harmony. Engage with the hive's entrances from peripheral angles, averting interference with their natural flight paths. Observing the bees' behavior vigilantly, a shift towards agitation alerts you to pause and allow smoke to subdue them further if necessary. Such practices harmonize inspections, facilitating a focus on the hive's wellbeing, rather than reactive measures to defensive bees.

Despite these efforts, stings may occur—it's an accepted, albeit unwelcome, facet of beekeeping. Acknowledging how to tend to stings is vital for maintaining comfort and composure. Avoid pinching the stinger out, as doing so could further release venom into the skin. Instead, employ a tool or fingernail to scrape it gently, as highlighted by experts (Source 2). Quick application of ice serves to mitigate swelling and numb the affected area, while antihistamines offer relief from the itch. For individuals with severe allergies, carrying an epinephrine auto-injector is an unequivocal must. Recognizing allergy symptoms and acting with a predefined safety plan ensures preparedness for urgent situations.

Interactive Element: Personal Protective Gear Checklist

Developing a comprehensive checklist before each hive inspection can be likened to preparing for a voyage. Items to include span from your bee suit, veil, gloves, and smoker to essentials like the hive tool.

Consistent references to this list reinforce thorough preparation, significantly reducing the chance of over-looked necessities.

With time and repeated experience, handling bees transitions into an intuitive dance of sorts. As familiarity builds, so does the ease in which you communicate with the hive. Beekeeping embodies a dual nature; on one hand, it concerns the tangible aspects of hive management, but on the other, it is an exploration into the nuanced language of bee behavior. Every engagement further deepens your linkage to these industrious insects, providing rich insights and fortifying your appreciation for the bee's complex and delicate world.

Navigating Local Beekeeping Regulations

Before setting up your own hive, it's crucial to understand the legal landscape that governs beekeeping in your area. Beekeeping regulations can vary widely, often depending on the specific characteristics of your locality. Typically, these regulations cover aspects like the number of hives you can maintain, the minimum distance they need to be from property lines, and measures to ensure public safety. Some regions might require beekeepers to register their hives, while others focus on zoning laws that dictate whether beekeeping is permissible in residential areas. This patchwork of rules ensures that beekeeping remains a harmonious activity, balancing the interests of beekeepers with those of the broader community.

Engaging with the bureaucratic process to obtain necessary permits can initially appear daunting. Yet, with a systematic approach, it becomes manageable. Start by visiting your local government or municipal website to gather information on specific beekeeping requirements. Often, these sites provide detailed guidelines or contact numbers for departments handling agricultural or environmental matters. Filling out applications accurately is vital, as incomplete submissions can delay the process. Be prepared to provide details about your planned hive location, the number of hives you intend to keep, and any measures you'll implement to mitigate potential issues like swarming or hive aggression. It's also beneficial to keep records of all communications and submissions, creating a paper trail that can be invaluable if questions arise later.

Staying informed about legal changes is equally important. Local regulations can evolve, reflecting new environmental concerns or shifting community attitudes towards urban agriculture. Subscribing to newsletters from local beekeeping associations or participating in community forums can keep you updated on any legislative amendments. Engaging with these networks not only informs you of rule changes but also connects you with fellow beekeepers who might share insights and experiences relevant to your practice. Being proactive in this regard ensures that your hobby remains compliant and sustainable over time.

For those seeking deeper understanding or facing complex regulatory challenges, various resources offer guidance and support. Local beekeeping clubs often have members well-versed in navigating legal intricacies, providing firsthand advice and mentorship. National organizations like the American Beekeeping Federation might offer broader insights and resources for best practices in compliance. Online platforms dedicated to beekeeping can also be treasure troves of information, featuring articles and discussions on legal topics pertinent to both novice and seasoned beekeepers. These resources empower you to approach beekeeping with confidence, armed with knowledge that safeguards both your bees and your standing within the community.

In addition to local resources, consider consulting legal professionals who specialize in agricultural law if your concerns extend beyond straightforward compliance. They can offer tailored advice, ensuring that your setup aligns with both current regulations and any anticipated changes. Such consultations are especially beneficial if you plan to expand your apiary or engage in commercial honey production, where legal nuances become more pronounced.

The journey into beekeeping is enriched by understanding and respecting these legal frameworks. They not only protect pollinators and people but also foster a supportive environment where urban agriculture can thrive alongside modern living. Each step taken towards compliance strengthens your role as a responsible steward of both bees and the environment they enrich. The knowledge gained through navigating these regulations enhances your capacity to contribute positively to local ecosystems, reinforcing the symbiotic relationship between humans and nature.

Ethical Beekeeping: Practices and Principles

The ethical treatment of bees stands not only as a cornerstone of sustainable beekeeping but also as a testament to our evolving understanding of our relationship with the natural world. It underscores the profound connection between human activity and ecological sustainability. Bees, though tiny in physical stature, are monumental in their ecological significance, providing essential services through their complex pollination processes. These intricate yet crucial interactions ensure the persistence of plant species that form the backbone of innumerable ecosystems around the globe. Thus, treating them with respect and care is not merely a choice but a compelling obligation. Ethical practices ensure that while we benefit from the fruits of their labor, we also respect their natural behaviors and fundamental needs. This mutually beneficial symbiotic relationship fosters healthier colonies that are better equipped to withstand the myriad environmental stresses they face.

Humane Hive Management

Humane hive management techniques form the bedrock of ethical beekeeping. Central to this approach is the unwavering focus on maintaining hive health without causing undue stress or harm to the bees themselves. Regular inspections should be gentle and minimally invasive, allowing you to monitor the colony's wellbeing without creating unnecessary disturbances to their daily activities. The key is to observe with respect, learning to read the bees' behavior and responding with care. When managing pests, prioritize natural methods over chemical treatments. Integrated Pest Management (IPM), for instance, combines biological controls with cultural practices to sustainably reduce pest populations. This method not only protects the bees but also shields the surrounding environment from chemical exposure and potentially harmful residues. By gaining a deep understanding and respect for the bees' natural life cycles, beekeepers can create favorable conditions that align with the bees' innate behaviors, thereby promoting a thriving and robust hive.

Transparency and Community Engagement

Transparency in beekeeping practices is another pivotal aspect of ethical management. Openly sharing information about how you manage your hives fosters trust within your community and among fellow beekeepers. This transparency extends to methods used for honey production, hive maintenance, and pest control strategies. By being open about your practices, you set a high standard for ethical behavior in the beekeeping community—one that encourages others to adopt similar sustainable practices. Additionally, engaging with your community through workshops or educational presentations can demystify beekeeping processes. Offering insight into practices can alleviate public concerns and promote a deeper understanding of the intricacies involved in beekeeping, fostering a collective commitment to bee welfare and ecological preservation.

Sustainable Practices in Beekeeping

Practicing ethical beekeeping involves adopting actionable steps that align with high standards of care and sustainability. One such practice involves ensuring that bees have access to diverse forage throughout the various seasons. Planting an assortment of flowering plants that bloom at different times provides a continuous and rich food source, supporting bee health and productivity. Another prudent practice is refraining from overharvesting honey. Leaving a sufficient amount of honey for the bees to sustain themselves during the winter months is crucial. This thoughtful consideration ensures that bees remain healthy throughout the year without becoming reliant on artificial feeding. Furthermore, providing natural shelters around your apiary can offer protection to hives from harsh or extreme weather conditions, thereby enhancing colony resilience.

A commitment to ethical practices also involves vigilance concerning bee health and adopting proactive measures to prevent disease spread. Regularly rotating hive locations can help in reducing parasite buildup in the soil, thereby decreasing the risk of pest infestations. Similarly, maintaining clean equipment helps minimize the transmission of diseases between hives. Equipping yourself with knowledge about bee diseases and their symptoms allows for early detection and intervention, thereby safeguarding the entire apiary from potential outbreaks. Additionally, supporting genetic diversity through the incorporation of locally adapted bee strains into your apiary strengthens the colony's resilience to diseases and environmental changes, enhancing the overall health of the bee community.

The Broader Impact of Ethical Beekeeping

By integrating these practices into daily beekeeping routines, you contribute positively to the broader environmental landscape. Ethical beekeeping nurtures not only the bees in your care but also the ecosystems they intimately interact with and inhabit. As stewards of these remarkable creatures, we wield the power and responsibility to shape a more sustainable future by adopting practices that prioritize bee welfare and ensure ecological harmony. The impact of ethical beekeeping extends far beyond individual hives, resonating throughout gardens, communities, and ecosystems at large, fostering a world where nature thrives symbiotically with human enterprise.

Dealing with Neighbor Concerns and Zoning Laws

Venturing into beekeeping in urban or suburban settings often means navigating a complex social landscape. Neighbors, understandably, may express concerns about the introduction of bees into close-knit communities. Commonly voiced apprehensions include the potential for increased stings, allergies, or swarming events. Some worry about the proximity of hives to shared spaces like gardens or patios. These concerns, while valid, can be mitigated through thoughtful dialogue and strategic planning. Addressing these issues with empathy and clear information can transform apprehension into support, fostering a community that values and supports urban beekeeping.

Effective communication forms the cornerstone of harmonious neighbor relations. Initiating open conversations about your beekeeping plans is crucial. Transparency about hive locations, management practices, and the ecological benefits of bees can ease fears and build trust. Consider organizing an informal meeting or presentation to share your enthusiasm for beekeeping, highlighting its role in supporting local biodiversity and garden health. Providing educational materials or inviting neighbors to observe hive activities can demystify the process, turning potential critics into allies. By fostering a dialogue rooted in mutual respect and understanding, you lay the groundwork for cooperation and goodwill.

Strategically placing hives to minimize disruption balances both the bees' needs and community comfort. When selecting a hive location, consider factors such as flight paths and natural barriers. Position hives away from high-traffic areas, using fences or hedges to direct bee movement skyward, reducing interactions with people. This placement not only ensures bee safety but also alleviates neighbor concerns about unexpected encounters. Urban environments may limit space, but creative solutions like rooftop gardens or secluded backyard corners can provide bees with a peaceful haven without encroaching on shared spaces.

Navigating zoning laws requires a proactive approach to ensure compliance with local regulations. Zoning laws dictate where beekeeping is permissible, often based on property size, hive numbers, and distance from property lines. Begin by researching local ordinances through city planning departments or municipal websites. Understanding these laws is pivotal in aligning your beekeeping practices with community standards. Engaging with local authorities early in the process can help clarify any ambiguities and streamline the compliance process. These interactions may also reveal opportunities for advocacy or policy change, benefiting both current and future beekeepers.

Compliance extends beyond initial setup; it involves ongoing engagement with regulatory bodies and community stakeholders. Regularly reviewing zoning changes ensures that your practices remain lawful as regulations evolve. Participating in local beekeeping associations provides a network of support and resources for navigating legal challenges. These groups often have members who are well-versed in local laws, offering insights and strategies for maintaining compliance. Involving yourself in these communities strengthens ties with fellow beekeepers, reinforcing a collective commitment to responsible and sustainable urban agriculture.

By addressing neighbor concerns, communicating effectively, strategically placing hives, and navigating zoning laws, urban beekeepers can create a supportive environment for their bees and community. This chapter has highlighted the importance of proactive engagement and thoughtful planning in overcoming challenges associated with urban beekeeping. As we move forward, the next chapter will delve into advanced hive management techniques that further optimize your beekeeping endeavors. By building on the foundation laid here, you'll continue to nurture thriving colonies that not only benefit your garden but also contribute to the health of our planet's ecosystems.

Chapter 7: Budget-Friendly Beekeeping

Affordable Hive Building: DIY Projects

As a child, I often marveled at how my grandfather could turn the most unassuming scraps of wood into something truly magnificent. His hands, weathered by years and years of toil and labor outdoors, deftly crafted hives using nothing more than a few basic tools and a practiced eye for detail. It was in the quiet afternoons by his side that I learned the value of resourcefulness and creativity, understanding that beekeeping need not be an expensive venture at all. Instead, it can be a fulfilling journey into self-sufficiency. Today, in our fast-paced world, taking the time to construct your own hive remains a delightful and cost-effective approach to starting your own apiary. Instead of purchasing ready-made and often costly hives, consider the enriching experience and satisfaction of building one yourself from scratch. Not only does this approach save money, but it also allows you to tailor each aspect of the hive to suit your specific needs and the unique environment in which you intend to place it.

Diving into DIY hive construction starts with choosing a design that perfectly fits your capabilities and goals. Understanding your local climate and landscape will inform your design choices, ensuring that your bees will thrive. The Langstroth hive, for instance, is a popular choice among many beekeepers, celebrated for its modular design and ease of use. Its adaptability has made it a paramount choice for beginners and experienced beekeepers alike. Building a Langstroth involves assembling a series of stackable boxes with removable frames inside, specifically designed to facilitate honey harvesting without disturbing the delicate balance within the hive. Begin by creating a solid, even, and stable base, which serves as the hive's foundation and cornerstone. Next, construct the brood boxes and honey supers, ensuring each piece fits snugly to prevent drafts and ensure optimal protection against the weather. Finish by meticulously adding an inner cover and a sturdy weatherproof outer cover to protect your hive from the elements. Each step in this process not only enhances your technical understanding of hive construction but also deepens your connection and dedication to the beekeeping craft, fostering a profound appreciation for the complexity of these fascinating creatures.

To embark on this fulfilling project, you'll need to gather some basic but essential tools and materials. Essential items include a trusty saw for cutting wood to precise measurements, a reliable hammer and nails for firmly securing the pieces during assembly, and a versatile drill for attaching crucial components. You'll also need untreated wood, such as pine or cedar, which naturally offer durability and resistance to decay. Consider using non-toxic wood preservatives to further extend the life of your hive, ensuring it remains a safe haven for your bees. Additionally, you'll require wire mesh to provide necessary ventilation and a protective coating like exterior-grade paint to shield against moisture and the elements. These materials form the backbone of your DIY hive, offering both practicality and protection for your bees as they establish their colony.

Creativity plays a pivotal role in reducing costs and minimizing environmental impact when sourcing materials for your new endeavor. Repurposing items like pallets or reclaimed lumber not only keeps expenses low but also supports sustainable practices by giving new life to old, unused materials. Old furniture pieces can be disassembled, reshaped, and transformed into practical hive components, while leftover exterior paint can provide much-needed protection against the elements without additional costs. Always ensure that any recycled materials are free from harmful chemicals or contaminants before incorporating them into your hive, thereby safeguarding your bees. This approach not only saves money but also fosters a spirit of innovation and resourcefulness in your beekeeping endeavors, echoing the natural cycle of renewal and transformation that bees themselves embody.

Interactive Element: DIY Hive Construction Checklist

Create a comprehensive checklist to meticulously guide your DIY hive project. Include each pivotal step of construction from base assembly to the final finishing touches, detailing out every intricate detail. List necessary tools and materials alongside their sources, ensuring you have everything prepared and ready before starting the actual construction. Regularly update this checklist as you progress, refining your process and gaining invaluable insights into ensuring success for future projects.

As you embark on this rewarding path of building your own hive, remember that each piece you carefully assemble brings you one step closer to deeply understanding the incredible and intricate world of bees. The immense satisfaction derived from watching a colony thrive in a hive crafted with your own hands is indeed immeasurable—a living testament to both your ingenuity and commitment to sustainable and thoughtful beekeeping practices.

Budgeting for Beekeeping: What to Expect

Starting your beekeeping adventure involves understanding and planning the financial aspect of this rewarding hobby. While the initial investment might seem daunting, a clear picture of what to expect can ease the journey. The startup costs typically include purchasing bees, hives, protective gear, and essential tools. A basic hive setup, like the Langstroth, can range from $200 to $300, depending on whether you buy it assembled or as a DIY kit. Bees themselves, whether packaged or as nucleus colonies, can cost between $100 and $150. Protective clothing, including a suit, gloves, and veil, usually runs around $100. Essential tools like a smoker and hive tool add another $50 to $75 to your budget. Considering all these elements, expect to spend about $500 to $700 initially.

Managing ongoing costs in beekeeping requires a strategic approach to ensure sustainability without breaking the bank. Regular expenses include feeding supplements during scarce seasons, replacing damaged equipment, and purchasing treatments for pests like Varroa mites. To minimize these costs, consider buying in bulk when possible or joining a local beekeeping club that offers discounts on supplies. Regular maintenance also helps extend the life of your equipment, reducing the need for frequent replacements. Another strategy involves learning basic pest control methods that use natural ingredients, cutting down on costly chemical treatments. By investing time in education and preventive care, you can keep your hives healthy and your expenses manageable.

Exploring financing options can further ease the financial burden of starting and maintaining your apiary. Some aspiring beekeepers consider small community loans or grants from organizations focused on supporting pollinator health and conservation efforts. Look into local agricultural grants or programs that offer funding for sustainable practices. Additionally, some equipment suppliers provide financing plans to spread out the initial costs over a more extended period. Crowdfunding platforms can also serve as an unexpected resource; sharing your project with friends and family might garner support from those interested in promoting local sustainability initiatives.

Let's explore a sample beekeeping budget to guide you through planning your finances effectively. Begin with a list of startup costs: Allocate around $250 for your hive setup, $125 for bees, and $100 for protective gear, totaling $475. Add $75 for tools and initial feeding supplies, bringing your initial investment to approximately $550. For ongoing expenses, budget about $100 annually for feeding and pest treatments. Set aside an additional $50 per year for unforeseen repairs or replacements. If you plan to expand your apiary in the future, consider earmarking funds each year toward new hives or colonies. Keeping a detailed record of expenditures helps track spending and identify areas where adjustments may be needed.

The key to successful budgeting lies in balancing quality with cost-effectiveness. Prioritize high-quality essentials like protective gear and hive bodies while opting for more budget-friendly options when it comes to accessories or non-essential items. Remember that investing wisely at the outset can save money in the long run by preventing issues related to poor-quality materials or inadequate equipment. As you settle into beekeeping, you'll develop a better sense of which aspects are worth spending more on and where savings can be made without compromising on quality.

Incorporating creativity into your budgeting approach can also yield significant savings. Consider partnerships with local farms or community gardens that might allow you to place hives on their property in exchange for honey or pollination services. This arrangement reduces land costs while fostering community relationships and promoting environmental stewardship. Another option is to collaborate with other beekeepers on bulk purchases of supplies, sharing resources and reducing individual expenses.

By taking a proactive approach to budgeting and exploring various cost-saving strategies, you can enjoy the benefits of beekeeping without financial strain. This hobby not only provides the tangible reward of honey but also offers a deeper connection to nature and the satisfaction of contributing positively to ecological health. Embracing the principles of resourcefulness and sustainability enriches both your life and the environment around you, making every dollar spent an investment in a more vibrant future.

Cost-Effective Hive Maintenance Tips

Maintaining your hives need not be a costly endeavor. Instead, it can be a rewarding practice that ensures the longevity of your apiary without breaking the bank. Routine maintenance tasks form the backbone of hive health, and performing these consistently can save substantial amounts in the long run. Regularly inspecting your hives for signs of wear and tear is crucial. Check for cracks or gaps in the woodwork that might allow pests or cold air to enter. A simple application of non-toxic wood preservative or paint can seal minor imperfections, extending the life of your hive components. Additionally, replace any broken frames immediately to prevent disruption in your bee colony's productivity. Keeping debris away from hive entrances and ensuring proper ventilation are simple yet effective habits that bolster hive health and improve bee resilience.

When sourcing supplies for hive upkeep, consider exploring local resources that may not be immediately obvious. Farmer's markets or agricultural fairs often have vendors selling beekeeping supplies at discounted prices. These venues provide opportunities to engage directly with sellers, allowing for negotiation and better deals. Online marketplaces and forums can also be treasure troves for affordable equipment, especially if you're open to purchasing gently used items. Be cautious, however, to check for signs of wear that might compromise functionality. Subscription services for beekeeping supplies can offer regular discounts and bundle deals, reducing the cost per item over time.

For common maintenance issues, DIY solutions can be both economical and effective. Pest control is a critical aspect of hive maintenance that often requires costly treatments if not managed proactively. Consider using natural deterrents like essential oils—such as lemongrass or peppermint—diluted in water and sprayed around the hive's exterior to ward off pests like ants and mites. These natural treatments are not only cost-effective but also environmentally friendly, posing no risk of chemical contamination to your bees or their honey. For insulation during colder months, old blankets or burlap sacks can be repurposed into wraps for hives, providing warmth without the expense of commercial insulation products.

The benefits of shared equipment and resources among beekeepers should not be underestimated. Joining a local beekeeping association or club can open doors to a wealth of shared knowledge and pooled resources. Many groups maintain communal equipment inventories, allowing members to borrow rather than purchase expensive items outright. This is particularly useful for specialized tools that are infrequently needed but crucial when required. Additionally, group buying opportunities can arise within these communities, where members collectively purchase supplies in bulk for significant savings.

Establishing a network with fellow beekeepers fosters an environment of mutual aid and innovation. Beyond just sharing physical resources, these connections offer a platform for exchanging tips and strategies that enhance hive management efficiency. This collaborative spirit not only reduces individual costs but also enriches your beekeeping experience through shared learning and support. By leveraging the collective wisdom and generosity within these communities, you can navigate challenges with confidence and creativity.

By incorporating these cost-effective strategies into your routine, you cultivate a sustainable approach to beekeeping that emphasizes resourcefulness and ingenuity. This pragmatic mindset ensures that you can maintain thriving hives without undue financial strain, allowing you to focus on the joys of beekeeping and the profound connection it fosters with nature. Each small adjustment or innovation strengthens your apiary's resilience, ensuring its success over the seasons.

Sourcing Bees and Equipment on a Budget

Finding affordable bee suppliers can feel like searching for a needle in a haystack, but with the right approach, you can source bees without draining your wallet. Begin by reaching out to local beekeeping associations or clubs; these communities often have connections with reputable suppliers who offer bees at competitive prices. Another viable option is to consider catching swarms during the swarming season, typically in spring. Swarming bees are looking for a new home and can be captured with minimal cost, often just the price of a swarm trap or a small reward for the property owner. Additionally, some beekeepers sell nucleus colonies or "nucs," which are small, established colonies that can jumpstart your beekeeping adventure with less risk than starting from packages of bees.

When it comes to equipment, purchasing new may not always be the best financial decision for those starting on a budget. Alternatives abound if you're open to exploring second-hand options. Check online marketplaces or local classified ads where fellow beekeepers often sell gently used gear at reduced prices. Be cautious with used equipment, however, especially when it comes to frames and combs, as these can harbor diseases that could jeopardize your hive's health. If you can verify the cleanliness and condition of these items, they can be a cost-effective way to acquire quality gear. Another option is to purchase unassembled equipment kits, which typically cost less than fully assembled hives. These kits provide the added benefit of familiarizing yourself with each component's function as you put them together.

Quality should never be sacrificed for quantity, especially in beekeeping. While it might be tempting to cut costs by opting for cheaper options, investing in high-quality essentials will save you money and headaches in the long run. Prioritize purchasing durable protective gear, such as bee suits and veils, which not only ensure your safety but also last longer with repeated use. Similarly, choose reliable smokers and hive tools, as these will be your constant companions during hive inspections. Skimping on these essentials could lead to frequent replacements or, worse, discourage you from continuing your beekeeping endeavors due to discomfort or inconvenience.

Negotiating and seeking discounts are valuable skills that can significantly reduce your beekeeping costs. When purchasing bees or equipment, don't hesitate to ask suppliers if they offer any discounts for bulk purchases or first-time buyers. Attend local beekeeping events or conferences, where vendors may provide special deals exclusive to attendees. Building relationships with suppliers and fellow beekeepers can also open doors to future discounts or shared resources. Additionally, keep an eye out for end-of-season sales or clearance events where equipment is often sold at a fraction of its usual price.

By carefully sourcing and selecting bees and equipment with budget considerations in mind, you set yourself up for success without compromising on quality or safety. Remember that investing wisely at the outset can prevent costly replacements down the road, allowing you to focus on nurturing your hives and enjoying the rewarding experience of beekeeping. As you continue your journey into this fascinating world, let resourcefulness guide you—seeking out opportunities to learn from others and adapt strategies that work best for your unique circumstances.

In this chapter, we've explored practical ways to source bees and equipment affordably while emphasizing quality over quantity. These strategies encourage creativity and community involvement, ensuring you can start and maintain your apiary without financial strain. In our next chapter, we'll delve into sustainable and organic beekeeping practices that align with environmental stewardship while enhancing hive health and productivity. Balancing budget-savvy approaches with ecological responsibility paves the way for a fulfilling and impactful beekeeping experience.

Chapter 8: Sustainable and Organic Beekeeping Practices

The Benefits of Organic Beekeeping

I remember my grandfather's hives, nestled among rows of orange, lemon, Ylang-ylang and other flowering and fruit-bearing trees, where the air was thick with the scent of citrus blooms and the soothing hum of bees. Even as a child, I sensed that the bees thrived not just on the nectar but on the care that eschewed chemicals and embraced nature's rhythms. Organic beekeeping, an echo of those timeless practices, offers a path that nurtures both bees and the environment. It allows us to cultivate colonies without exposing them to synthetic chemicals, promoting healthier hives and more resilient bees. This approach decreases the bees' susceptibility to diseases and parasites, which are often exacerbated by chemical residues in traditional apiaries. By adopting organic methods, you minimize stress within your colonies, supporting their natural immune responses and fostering healthier populations.

The purity of organic honey and hive products stands as a testament to these practices. Free from chemical residues, organic honey captures the essence of floral diversity, offering a more authentic taste that reflects the terroir of your landscape. This purity extends to other hive products like beeswax and propolis, which are highly valued for their natural properties and enhanced marketability. Consumers increasingly seek out these products for their perceived health benefits and environmental credentials. Organic honey commands a premium price in markets that value sustainability and quality, providing added financial incentives for beekeepers committed to these practices.

For beekeepers, the transition to organic methods can yield numerous benefits beyond healthier hives. By eliminating chemical inputs, you reduce costs associated with synthetic treatments and pesticides. This shift enhances your peace of mind, knowing that your practices align with a commitment to environmental stewardship. Furthermore, you foster a deeper connection with your bees and their environment, cultivating an understanding of their natural cycles and behaviors. This knowledge empowers you to make informed decisions that support both hive health and ecological balance.

Consumers also benefit from organic beekeeping through access to high-quality, sustainably produced honey and hive products. As awareness of environmental issues grows, more people are seeking products that align with their values. Organic honey not only meets this demand but also contributes to broader ecological efforts by supporting practices that prioritize biodiversity and habitat conservation. When consumers choose organic products, they actively participate in a cycle that promotes sustainable agriculture and environmental responsibility.

The ecological advantages of organic beekeeping extend far beyond the boundaries of your apiary. By avoiding synthetic chemicals, you contribute to healthier soils and waterways, reducing pollution and preserving natural habitats for countless species. This approach supports biodiversity by encouraging diverse plant life and providing essential resources for other pollinators like butterflies and solitary bees. The ripple effect of these practices enhances the resilience of local ecosystems, creating landscapes where nature thrives in harmony.

Interactive Element: Reflection on Organic Practices

Consider setting aside time in your journal to reflect on how organic beekeeping aligns with your values and goals. How do these practices resonate with your vision for a sustainable future? Document any changes you notice in your hives or garden as you adopt organic methods. Reflect on the impact these changes have on your relationship with your bees and the broader environment.

As you explore the benefits of organic beekeeping, embrace the opportunity to innovate and adapt your practices in ways that honor both tradition and modern understanding. By cultivating hives that thrive without chemical intervention, you contribute to a legacy of stewardship that respects the delicate balance between human activity and natural ecosystems. Through organic beekeeping, you join a community dedicated to nurturing the planet while enjoying the bountiful rewards of healthy hives and pure, natural honey.

Sustainable Hive Management Practices

Sustainable hive management hinges on reducing resource consumption without sacrificing productivity. One effective strategy involves optimizing your hive's energy efficiency. By carefully selecting the location of your hives, you can leverage natural sunlight and windbreaks to create a stable microclimate. This reduces the bees' need to expend energy on temperature regulation. Additionally, consider using insulated hive designs that maintain warmth in winter and coolness in summer. This not only conserves bee energy but also minimizes your reliance on supplemental feeding, as bees will have more energy to forage. Efficient resource use extends to water management as well. By installing a rainwater collection system, you can provide bees with a consistent water source, reducing the need for frequent refills and conserving a vital resource.

Waste reduction within the apiary is another critical aspect of sustainability. Start by reevaluating your use of disposable materials. Opt for reusable or biodegradable options whenever possible, such as wooden frames instead of plastic ones. When it comes to hive maintenance, repurpose old wax by melting it down and forming new foundation sheets or candles. Beeswax is a versatile material that can be recycled within the apiary, reducing waste and creating new products. Additionally, consider composting organic waste from hive cleanings. This not only minimizes landfill contributions but also enriches your garden soil, creating a natural cycle of waste reduction and resource renewal.

Local sourcing plays a pivotal role in sustainable beekeeping. By obtaining supplies and bees from nearby sources, you significantly reduce your carbon footprint associated with transportation. Locally sourced bees are often better adapted to the local environment, increasing their chances of thriving. Similarly, purchasing equipment from local craftsmen supports the community and ensures that materials are suited to your specific climate conditions. This approach strengthens local economies and fosters a sense of community among beekeepers.

Creating a closed-loop beekeeping system seamlessly integrates with other sustainable practices. Imagine combining beekeeping with permaculture principles, where every element of your system supports the others. Planting bee-friendly crops not only provides sustenance for your bees but also enhances soil fertility through natural pollination processes. In return, bees boost the productivity of these crops, creating a harmonious cycle of mutual benefit. Consider integrating chickens into your system; they can help control pests by foraging around hives while providing you with fresh eggs. This closed-loop approach maximizes resource use and minimizes waste, creating a resilient and self-sustaining ecosystem.

Reflect on how sustainable practices align with broader environmental goals. Consider the impact of your beekeeping choices on local biodiversity and ecosystem health. By implementing these strategies, you contribute to a larger movement toward environmental stewardship and resilience. Each small change you make— whether it's reducing waste or sourcing locally—cumulatively impacts the health of our planet.

Visual Element: Sustainable Beekeeping Flowchart

Imagine a flowchart illustrating the interconnected elements of sustainable beekeeping. It begins with hive placement, branching into energy-efficient designs and water conservation systems. From there, it leads to waste reduction strategies like composting and wax recycling, which loop back into soil enrichment and resource renewal. The chart highlights local sourcing at its heart, connecting all elements to create a closed-loop system that supports both bees and the environment.

By embracing these sustainable hive management practices, you not only nurture healthier colonies but also steward the environment they depend on. Through thoughtful resource management, waste reduction, and local engagement, you craft an apiary that thrives in harmony with nature's rhythms. As you delve deeper into these practices, you'll find that each step taken toward sustainability echoes far beyond your hives, contributing to a flourishing world where bees—and all life—can thrive.

Using Natural Remedies for Hive Health

In my early days of beekeeping, I watched intently as my grandfather tended to the hives, his hands moving with a gentle precision born from years of experience. He often eschewed synthetic chemicals, instead opting for remedies that were as natural as the bees themselves. This approach not only respected the delicate balance of nature but also cultivated healthier and more resilient colonies. Today, more beekeepers are turning to organic solutions to manage common hive issues, finding that these methods offer effective alternatives to chemical treatments.

Natural remedies can address a variety of hive challenges, from pest control to disease prevention. Essential oils, for instance, serve as powerful allies in maintaining hive health. Thyme oil, renowned for its efficacy against Varroa mites, can be applied by mixing a few drops into sugar syrup or placing soaked pads within the hive. This disrupts the mites' reproduction without harming the bees. Similarly, lemongrass oil acts as an attractant and calming agent, aiding in swarm management while promoting a peaceful hive environment.

Herbal infusions and teas offer another layer of protection. Chamomile and peppermint teas, when cooled and sprayed within the hive, can deter pests like wax moths and small hive beetles. These natural deterrents create an inhospitable environment for pests while remaining gentle on bees. Additionally, garlic extract has shown promise in bolstering bees' immune systems, providing resilience against bacterial infections. A diluted solution can be mixed with sugar syrup and fed to the bees during periods of stress or disease susceptibility.

The application of these remedies requires a thoughtful approach to ensure effectiveness. Timing is crucial; applying treatments during periods of low brood production enhances their impact while minimizing stress on the colony. Consistency is key as well—regular applications may be necessary to achieve desired results. Observing your bees closely after introducing a remedy allows you to gauge its effectiveness and adjust as needed. Monitoring for signs of improvement or adverse reactions ensures that your efforts support rather than hinder the hive's well-being.

Integrating natural remedies into your beekeeping practices yields numerous benefits. This approach aligns with a broader commitment to sustainability by reducing reliance on synthetic chemicals that can harm both bees and the environment. It fosters a deeper understanding of your hives, encouraging you to observe and respond to their needs with care and intuition. Over time, you'll notice healthier colonies with increased resilience against common challenges, resulting in more productive hives and higher-quality honey.

To assist you in exploring these remedies, consider a reference guide detailing common natural solutions and their applications. For Varroa mite control, thyme oil and powdered sugar dusting are effective options. For immune support, garlic extract and herbal teas such as chamomile or peppermint can be introduced. Wax moth prevention might include cedar wood shavings or neem oil, while propolis tinctures can act as antibacterial agents within the hive.

The journey into natural beekeeping invites you to reconnect with age-old practices that honor both bees and their environment. As you experiment with these remedies, you'll find that each method enhances your understanding of the intricate balance that sustains thriving hives. By prioritizing natural solutions, you contribute not only to healthier bees but also to a healthier planet—a legacy that reflects the timeless wisdom of those who tended hives long before us.

The path of natural beekeeping is one of discovery and adaptation. Your role as a beekeeper becomes that of a steward and guardian, fostering an environment where bees can flourish without chemical interference. This approach nurtures both your hives and your own understanding of the delicate interplay between nature and nurture. With each remedy you apply, you strengthen the bond between yourself and your bees, cultivating a harmonious relationship that benefits all involved.

Minimizing Environmental Impact in Beekeeping

Reflecting on my early days in beekeeping, I often think about the delicate balance between our actions and the natural world. This balance becomes evident when we consider the environmental footprint of our beekeeping activities. Reducing our ecological impact is not merely a choice; it's a responsibility that shapes the future of our ecosystems. One of the most effective strategies is to adopt practices that minimize energy consumption. By utilizing solar-powered equipment for hive monitoring and lighting, you can significantly cut down on electricity use. These small changes lead to substantial savings in resources over time.

Moreover, reducing the use of synthetic materials in your beekeeping setup makes a considerable difference. Opt for natural materials such as wood or straw for hive construction, which are biodegradable and less harmful to the environment. These materials not only blend seamlessly with the natural surroundings but also provide a healthier environment for your bees. Additionally, implementing water conservation techniques, like capturing rainwater for hive maintenance, reduces the demand on local water supplies, preserving this vital resource for other wildlife and plants.

The conversation about habitat conservation is ongoing and crucial. Bees thrive best in environments that offer diverse flora and natural nesting sites. By protecting existing habitats and restoring degraded ones, you create sanctuaries for bees to flourish. Planting native flowers and trees around your apiary creates corridors that support not just bees but a variety of pollinators and wildlife. These plants act as buffers, enhancing biodiversity while providing essential resources throughout the year. In urban areas, advocating for green spaces and community gardens helps counteract concrete sprawl, creating oases where nature can rejuvenate.

Understanding the relationship between beekeeping and climate change underscores the importance of sustainable practices. Climate change alters blooming cycles, disrupts weather patterns, and affects bee behavior. Sustainable beekeeping can mitigate some of these impacts by encouraging biodiversity and resilience within local ecosystems. Practicing crop rotation and interplanting diverse species not only supports bee health but also improves soil quality, promoting carbon sequestration and reducing greenhouse gas emissions. These practices create resilient systems that adapt better to changing climates, supporting both bees and human communities.

Examples of successful sustainability initiatives abound in the beekeeping world. Consider a collective of urban beekeepers who transformed rooftops into thriving green spaces, integrating solar panels and rain gardens alongside hives. This initiative not only provided habitats for bees but also reduced the urban heat island effect, demonstrating how creative solutions can address multiple environmental challenges simultaneously. In rural areas, some beekeepers have partnered with farmers to establish pollinator-friendly buffer zones around fields. These zones enhance crop yields while providing habitat for bees and other wildlife, creating a win-win situation for agriculture and conservation.

Another successful case involves a beekeeper who collaborated with local schools to create educational programs focused on sustainability. By engaging students in hands-on workshops and apiary visits, they fostered awareness and inspired a new generation of environmentally conscious citizens. These programs emphasized the interconnectedness of ecosystems, illustrating how individual actions contribute to broader conservation efforts.

As we wrap up this chapter on minimizing environmental impact in beekeeping, it's clear that each decision we make ripples through the environment. By adopting sustainable practices, we safeguard not only our hives but also the intricate web of life that sustains us all. In our next chapter, we'll explore advanced hive design techniques that further enhance productivity and efficiency while maintaining harmony with nature's rhythms. This journey into innovative solutions promises to enrich your beekeeping experience and deepen your connection to the natural world.

Chapter 9: Enhancing the Beekeeping Experience

Stories from Experienced Beekeepers

In the heart of a buzzing apiary, where the air hums with purpose and life, each beekeeper finds their own unique story woven through the threads of experience and discovery. One such tale is from a seasoned beekeeper named Lydia, who found solace and joy through the rhythm of tending to her hives. Lydia recalls her initial hesitance, standing before her first hive with both trepidation and anticipation. Despite her fears, she chose to lean into the hum of the bees, finding a sense of calm and focus that only grew with time. Over the years, she learned the subtle art of reading the mood of a hive—a skill that comes only with patience and dedication. This intuitive connection with her bees became a form of meditation, teaching her to move with intention and serenity.

In another part of the world, a different beekeeper named Arjun recounts his journey from novice to mentor. Arjun started with a single hive in his small urban garden, motivated by a desire to contribute to local biodiversity. His early days were filled with trial and error as he navigated the challenges of urban beekeeping. Through persistence, he learned to adapt his practices to suit his environment, implementing creative solutions like vertical gardens to maximize space. As his hives multiplied, so did his confidence and understanding of bee behavior. Arjun found himself sharing his knowledge with others, hosting workshops in community gardens and mentoring new beekeepers. This role brought him immense fulfillment, as he witnessed the spark of curiosity and passion ignite in others.

Memorable moments in a beekeeper's life often revolve around milestones that mark growth and achievement. For Emily, a highlight was her first successful honey harvest. After months of nurturing her bees through unpredictable weather and learning to navigate their complex social dynamics, she finally tasted the fruits of her labor—a rich, golden honey with notes of wildflowers from her garden. This moment was not just about the honey itself; it symbolized her journey from uncertainty to proficiency, affirming her bond with the natural world. Each jar of honey she shared with friends and family became a testament to her dedication and perseverance.

Beekeeping is more than an activity; it's a catalyst for personal growth and transformation. Many beekeepers find that tending to hives cultivates patience, resilience, and mindfulness. The act of caring for bees demands attention to detail and an appreciation for life's small wonders. Through observing the intricate workings of a hive, beekeepers develop a deeper understanding of interconnectedness and the delicate balance of ecosystems. This perspective often extends beyond the apiary, influencing how they engage with the world and fostering a greater sense of stewardship for the environment.

Seasoned beekeepers offer invaluable insights that can guide newcomers on their path. One piece of advice frequently shared is the importance of continuous learning. Beekeeping is an ever-evolving practice, where each season brings new challenges and opportunities for knowledge. Experienced keepers recommend staying curious, attending workshops, and reading extensively to stay informed about advancements in bee health and management techniques. Another tip is to cultivate patience; bees operate on their own timeline, and rushing them can disrupt their harmony. Observing without interference allows beekeepers to learn from their bees' natural rhythms.

Reflection Section

Take a moment to reflect on your motivations for beekeeping. What drew you to this practice? What do you hope to learn or achieve? Consider keeping a journal where you document your observations, challenges, and successes as you progress on your beekeeping journey.

The stories shared by experienced beekeepers illuminate the diverse paths one can take within this practice. They remind us that beekeeping is not just about the hives or honey—it's a journey of growth, connection, and discovery that enriches our lives in ways we might never anticipate.

Engaging the Family: Beekeeping as a Shared Experience

Beekeeping opens a door to a world buzzing with life and learning that can engage the entire family. Imagine weekends spent together, hands-on, exploring the wonders of a hive. For families, this activity offers more than just honey—it offers opportunities for bonding and discovery. Younger children can participate by helping with simple tasks like painting hive boxes or observing bees through a safe distance. They might enjoy drawing pictures of what they see or keeping a journal of bee activity. Older kids and teens can take on more responsibility, learning to identify different types of bees and assisting with hive inspections under supervision. Introducing family members to the hive's rhythmic life fosters curiosity and respect for these incredible pollinators, making every visit an educational adventure.

The educational benefits for children involved in beekeeping are expansive. It provides a living lesson in biology, ecology, and environmental stewardship. Kids witness firsthand the intricate social structures within a hive—an entire microcosm of cooperation and productivity. They learn about the lifecycle of bees, from egg to adult, and gain insights into the essential role these creatures play in pollinating plants. Such knowledge encourages a deeper understanding of ecosystems and the importance of biodiversity. Beekeeping also builds valuable skills such as observation, patience, and problem-solving. As they engage with this process, children develop critical thinking abilities that apply beyond the apiary. This hands-on learning complements traditional education, providing practical experiences that spark curiosity and inspire lifelong learning.

Many families find that beekeeping strengthens their bonds, creating cherished memories and shared experiences. Take the story of the Martinez family, who started with a single hive in their backyard. Over time, their apiary grew, becoming a focal point for family gatherings. Each member developed their own connection with the bees—whether it was through harvesting honey or crafting beeswax candles. The process became a family tradition, something they looked forward to each season. The shared responsibility fostered teamwork, while the successes and challenges provided opportunities for communication and mutual support. Beekeeping became a thread that wove their stories together, enhancing their relationships in unexpected ways.

Balancing beekeeping with family life requires some planning but offers rich rewards. Start by designating specific times for beekeeping activities that fit into your family's schedule, perhaps setting aside a weekend morning or evening when everyone is available. Create a calendar of tasks and involve family members in planning sessions so everyone knows what to expect. Flexibility is key; be prepared to adjust plans based on weather conditions or hive needs. Encourage open communication about roles and responsibilities to ensure everyone feels included and valued. Remember to celebrate the small victories together—a successful hive inspection or the first honey harvest—turning these moments into family milestones.

Incorporating beekeeping into daily routines can also enhance family life. Use beekeeping-related tasks as opportunities for learning and growth. For example, meal times can include discussions about the importance of pollinators or ideas for bee-friendly garden projects. Encourage children to research bee topics that interest them, perhaps even turning these into school projects or presentations. Consider creating a family scrapbook or digital photo album to document your beekeeping journey together. This can be a fun way to look back on your progress and celebrate your collective achievements over time.

Beekeeping as a shared experience not only enriches family life but also instills values of sustainability and environmental responsibility in future generations. By involving your family in this rewarding practice, you foster a connection to nature that can inspire lifelong appreciation and care for the world around us. Through exploration and collaboration, you create lasting memories and bonds that transcend the seasons, much like the enduring cycles of the bees themselves.

Interactive Exercises for Aspiring Beekeepers

Engaging directly with the hive can transform your understanding of beekeeping from theory to practice. By rolling up your sleeves and diving into hands-on activities, you start to build not just knowledge, but confidence too. Begin with exercises that involve inspecting the hive. Approach your hives calmly, observing the bees' behavior as they move in and out. Take note of their patterns—are they bringing in pollen? Is there a cluster at the entrance? This kind of mindful observation sharpens your awareness and helps you interpret the hive's health. Next, challenge yourself with queen spotting. The queen is the heart of the hive, and learning to identify her amidst thousands of bees is a skill that both tests and improves your focus. Practice by gently lifting frames and scanning for her longer abdomen and distinct movements. Over time, this exercise becomes second nature, enhancing your efficiency and making inspections smoother.

To deepen your understanding, tackle some problem-solving scenarios. Imagine you're faced with a hive showing signs of Varroa mite infestation. What steps will you take to address the issue? Create a plan that includes monitoring mite levels using a sugar shake or alcohol wash, followed by implementing integrated pest management strategies. These could range from using screened bottom boards to introducing drone comb removal. Such exercises not only reinforce your knowledge but also prepare you for real-world challenges. Similarly, consider what actions you'd take if your bees showed signs of swarming. Develop a strategy that includes adding additional supers or performing a split to give your bees more space. These problem-solving activities encourage critical thinking and help you apply what you've learned in practical ways.

Incorporating quizzes and self-assessments into your routine can also be highly beneficial. After reading a chapter or completing an activity, take a moment to quiz yourself on key points. Questions like, "What are the signs of a healthy brood pattern?" or "How do you safely introduce a new queen?" test your retention and highlight areas needing more focus. Self-assessments can be informal but should push you to evaluate your strengths and areas for improvement. Did you struggle with identifying specific bee behaviors during an inspection? Recognize this as an opportunity to revisit those concepts. This reflective process is crucial for continuous learning and growth.

Journaling serves as a powerful tool for reflection and personal growth in beekeeping. By documenting your experiences, you create a personal record that allows you to track progress and reflect on lessons learned. Start by jotting down details after each hive visit: the weather conditions, bee behavior, any challenges faced, and how you addressed them. Note any changes in hive activity over time and hypothesize potential causes or solutions. Over weeks and months, this journal becomes a valuable resource—a chronicle of your journey that provides insight into patterns and trends in your apiary. It fosters a deeper connection with your bees and enhances your intuition in managing them.

Additionally, consider setting personal goals within your journaling practice. Perhaps you aim to increase honey yield by a certain percentage or reduce hive disturbances during inspections. Outline these aspirations clearly, along with actionable steps to achieve them. Revisit these goals regularly, adjusting strategies as needed based on new insights gained through experience or study. This practice not only keeps you focused but also instills a sense of accomplishment as you achieve milestones along the way.

Interactive learning, through hands-on exercises, problem-solving challenges, quizzes, and journaling, enriches the beekeeping experience by making it more personal and engaging. As you actively participate in these activities, you build a strong foundation of skills that enhance both your confidence and competence in managing hives effectively.

Building a Beekeeping Community

Connecting with fellow beekeepers opens up a world of shared knowledge and camaraderie that can elevate your beekeeping experience. When you join a community, you step into a space where ideas flow freely, challenges are met with collective wisdom, and success is celebrated together. The benefits of being part of such a community are manifold. You gain access to a wealth of experience from seasoned beekeepers who have weathered the ups and downs of hive management. The exchange of tips and techniques can help refine your skills, while discussions on trends and innovations keep you abreast of developments in the field. Beyond practical knowledge, there's an emotional support system—a network of individuals who understand the unique joys and challenges that come with nurturing bees.

Finding and joining local groups is a straightforward process, often beginning with a quick online search for beekeeping clubs or associations in your area. Many regions have established clubs that host regular meetings, workshops, and social events. These gatherings are excellent opportunities for networking and learning. You might also find online forums or social media groups dedicated to beekeeping, where you can engage with others from the comfort of your home. Consider attending local agricultural fairs or farmers' markets where beekeepers showcase their honey and products. These events often have information booths with details about joining local clubs. Once you find a group that aligns with your interests, dive in with an open mind and a willingness to contribute.

The formation of support networks among beekeepers is crucial for fostering a sense of belonging and mutual aid. These networks operate on the principle of reciprocity, where members offer help and guidance to one another. Whether it's advice on tackling pest issues or simply lending an ear during challenging times, support networks strengthen the collective resilience of the beekeeping community. Establishing such networks can be as simple as exchanging contact information with fellow beekeepers at workshops or meetings. Encourage regular communication through group chats or messaging apps, where members can share updates, ask questions, and offer assistance. Building these connections creates a safety net that bolsters individual efforts while enhancing the overall health of local bee populations.

Community-driven projects highlight the power of collective action in beekeeping. These initiatives often bring together diverse groups of people united by a common goal: to support bees and their ecosystems. For example, a group might collaborate on creating pollinator-friendly gardens in public spaces, which not only benefits the environment but also raises awareness about the importance of bees. In another instance, a community might organize educational programs for schools, introducing children to the fascinating world of bees through interactive demonstrations. Such projects foster a spirit of collaboration and shared responsibility, demonstrating how small contributions can lead to significant positive impacts.

A particularly inspiring story comes from a town where local beekeepers partnered with city officials to establish urban apiaries. The project involved transforming unused rooftops into thriving bee habitats, showcasing how urban spaces can support biodiversity. The initiative was well-received by the community, sparking interest in sustainable practices and prompting discussions on broader environmental topics. This project not only provided vital forage for bees but also fostered a sense of pride among residents who witnessed the transformation of their cityscape.

As you immerse yourself in the beekeeping community, remember that each interaction contributes to something greater than individual hives. You're part of a movement that champions sustainability, environmental stewardship, and education. The connections you build today lay the foundation for future collaborations that will benefit both people and bees alike.

In summary, engaging with the beekeeping community enriches your journey by providing access to shared knowledge, support networks, and collective initiatives. As we move forward into the next chapter, we'll explore innovative hive designs that enhance productivity and sustainability, continuing our exploration of how thoughtful practices can lead to thriving apiaries.

Chapter 10: Troubleshooting and Problem Solving

Identifying and Addressing Hive Diseases

Imagine standing at the edge of your apiary, the sun casting a warm glow on your hives, and feeling an unsettling sense of quiet. The usual energetic buzzing that fills the air, a melody of activity and purpose, is subdued, hinting at potential issues lurking within. Such a scenario, familiar to many seasoned beekeepers, serves as a poignant reminder of the profound importance of recognizing and addressing hive diseases with precision and timeliness. Just as a diligent gardener keeps a watchful eye for signs of wilting or discoloration in plants, understanding that these can be early indicators of underlying stresses or imbalances, so too must a beekeeper remain vigilant for subtle signs of hive distress and disruption.

Common hive diseases pose significant threats to bee colonies, and they demand an observant and informed approach. American foulbrood (AFB) is one of the most formidable foes, caused by a resilient bacterium that can spread insidiously through spores, surviving for decades in contaminated equipment or the environment. Infected larvae darken and decay into a rancid, odorous mass, a tell-tale sign for the knowledgeable beekeeper. **European foulbrood (EFB)**, while generally less virulent, nonetheless weakens colonies, with larvae displaying a twisted and contorted appearance in their cells. Another prevalent disease is **chalkbrood**, where fungal spores germinate in vulnerable larvae, effectively turning them into brittle, chalky mummies. Nosema, a gut parasite similar to a silent saboteur, causes dysentery and significantly reduces productivity and vitality. Recognizing these symptoms—be it unusual brood patterns, unexpected discoloration, or telltale spotting at the hive's entrance—is essential for timely intervention and effective management.

Prevention remains the cornerstone of successful disease management, emphasizing proactive measures to sustain hive health and vitality. Regularly scheduled inspections are invaluable, allowing for early detection of even the subtlest abnormalities and enabling swift corrective action. Prioritize impeccable hygiene by diligently sterilizing equipment and employing clean tools, thereby minimizing the risk of cross-contamination. Rotate frames with regularity to disrupt potential disease cycles and remove older combs that may harbor latent pathogens. Ensure that hives are well-ventilated and that moisture buildup is minimized to deter fungal growth, a common precursor to various afflictions. Selecting disease-resistant bee strains, which may inherit genetic defenses against certain pathogens, can further bolster colony resilience. Accentuating these efforts, a well-nourished colony with diverse forage access is inherently less vulnerable to stress-induced maladies.

Once a hive shows definitive signs of infection, prompt treatment becomes crucial. For the dreaded AFB, burning infected frames and equipment is often necessary due to the bacterium's formidable spore-forming nature. In contrast, EFB can frequently be managed with targeted antibiotics under veterinary guidance, although often, simply improving the overall colony conditions is sufficient to curtail its impact. Chalkbrood typically resolves by enhancing ventilation and reducing ambient humidity, creating a less hospitable environment for the fungus. For Nosema, administering Fumagillin B provides needed relief, though maintaining robust overall colony health remains the gold standard of defense. Always follow treatment protocols meticulously to avoid unintended harm to beneficial hive components, preserving the intricate balance of the hive's ecosystem.

Early detection and swift intervention are integral to preventing disease spread within and between colonies. Conduct regular and thorough brood pattern inspections, noting any irregularities or sudden discoloration. Act promptly if symptoms are detected—any delay exacerbates problems and complicates recovery efforts. Implement quarantine measures for affected hives to effectively contain potential outbreaks. Maintain detailed records of inspections and treatments, providing a comprehensive view that can track progress and inform future management decisions with a clarity borne from experience.

Reflection Section: Journaling for Hive Health

Consider keeping a detailed journal dedicated to documenting hive health observations in depth. Record symptoms noticed during meticulous inspections, actions taken in response, and subsequent treatment outcomes. Reflect on emerging patterns over time to refine your diagnostic skills and enhance the efficacy of your preventive strategies.

As you traverse the myriad challenges posed by hive diseases, remember that each decisive action taken contributes to the broader, essential endeavor of nurturing resilient hives capable of flourishing amidst adversity. Your attentive care and dedicated efforts are rewarded with vibrant, dynamic colonies that not only produce abundant honey but also play an indispensable role in supporting thriving garden ecosystems and promoting biodiversity.

Managing Weather-Related Challenges

Weather, with its capricious nature, can pose a myriad of challenges to bee colonies, impacting their health and productivity in ways both subtle and profound. A sudden drop in temperature or an unexpected storm can disrupt the delicate balance within a hive, leading to stress and reduced activity. Bees, being ectothermic creatures, depend heavily on external temperatures to regulate their internal processes. In colder climates, prolonged periods of low temperatures can cause bees to cluster tightly, conserving heat but limiting their foraging activity. This restriction often leads to insufficient food stores and increased susceptibility to diseases due to inactivity. Conversely, extreme heat can drive bees to leave the hive in search of water, diverting their energy from honey production and brood care. Rainy seasons further complicate matters by reducing foraging opportunities, leaving hives vulnerable to starvation and stress. Understanding these weather impacts is crucial for any beekeeper aiming to maintain thriving colonies that withstand nature's whims.

To shield hives from adverse weather, practical solutions must be implemented with foresight and adaptability. Insulating hives during cold spells can help maintain stable temperatures inside, reducing the energy bees expend to keep warm. Wrapping hives with breathable materials like burlap provides an effective barrier against the cold without suffocating the bees. Meanwhile, elevating hives on sturdy stands prevents moisture buildup from ground-level dampness, which can lead to rot and mildew. During hot spells, providing shade is vital. Positioning hives under trees or installing shade cloths can significantly reduce internal temperatures, preventing bees from overheating and preserving their energy for more productive activities. Ventilation plays a pivotal role in regulating hive temperatures as well. Ensuring adequate airflow by adjusting entrance reducers or installing screened bottom boards can alleviate heat stress while maintaining a comfortable environment for the colony.

Seasonal adjustments in hive management practices are essential to accommodate shifting weather patterns throughout the year. In spring, as temperatures rise and flowers bloom, bees become more active, requiring increased space within the hive to accommodate expanding populations. Adding supers during this time prevents overcrowding and encourages honey storage. Conversely, autumn calls for consolidation as bees prepare for winter. Reducing hive entrances minimizes drafts and fortifies the hive against intruding pests seeking refuge from the cold. Additionally, fall provides an opportune moment to assess food stores and supplement them if necessary, ensuring that bees enter winter with ample resources to survive until spring's arrival. Timing these adjustments to align with seasonal shifts ensures that bees remain robust and resilient against the challenges posed by fluctuating weather.

Location-specific strategies are paramount when tailoring management practices to regional climates, recognizing that different areas present unique challenges requiring customized approaches. In regions prone to heavy snowfall, beekeepers must prioritize snow clearance around hives to prevent blocked entrances and ensure consistent ventilation. Conversely, in areas experiencing monsoon rains, elevating hives and installing drainage systems can mitigate flooding risks and protect colonies from water damage. Arid environments necessitate a focus on providing water sources within proximity to hives, reducing the distance bees must travel in search of hydration during dry spells. Collaborating with local beekeeping associations can offer valuable insights into region-specific tactics that have proven successful over time.

A thorough understanding of weather-related challenges and their impact on bee colonies empowers beekeepers to implement effective strategies that safeguard hive health and productivity. By recognizing the influence of temperature fluctuations, rain patterns, and seasonal changes, you can make informed decisions that enhance colony resilience against nature's unpredictability. With proactive measures such as insulation, ventilation adjustments, and strategic positioning, your hives can thrive amidst diverse weather conditions. Adapting your approach based on regional climates further refines your ability to mitigate risks and optimize outcomes. As you continue to navigate these complexities, your commitment to understanding and responding to weather-driven challenges will undoubtedly yield rewards in the form of robust hives teeming with life and productivity.

Enhancing Hive Productivity: Tips and Tricks

Imagine standing before your hives on a warm summer day, the air thick with the hum of busy bees weaving between flowers, each carrying tiny golden parcels of pollen. This scene is not just a testament to the wonders of nature but also a reflection of a well-managed hive. Several factors play into hive productivity, and understanding these variables allows you to fine-tune your approach for optimal results. The genetic makeup of your bee colony is one critical factor; some strains, like the Italian or Carniolan bees, are renowned for their prolific honey production and gentle nature. The queen's health and vigor also play a pivotal role, as a robust queen will lay more eggs, leading to a larger workforce ready to gather nectar and maintain hive operations. Additionally, forage availability around your apiary significantly influences productivity. A diverse array of flowering plants provides the necessary nectar and pollen throughout the seasons, ensuring that bees have continuous food sources to support their energetic activities.

Maximizing honey production involves not only understanding these factors but also implementing strategic practices that boost efficiency and yield. Begin by ensuring your hives are positioned optimally, with entrances facing southeast to capture morning sun, which encourages early foraging. Regularly inspect the hive during peak nectar flow to prevent overcrowding—a common cause of swarming—by adding extra supers when necessary. This not only provides additional storage space but also reduces hive congestion, allowing bees to focus on honey production rather than relocation. Use queen excluders wisely; these devices prevent the queen from laying eggs in honey supers, ensuring that harvested frames are filled with pure honey, free from brood. When it comes to harvesting, timing is everything. Extract honey after at least 80% of the frames have capped cells; this ensures the moisture content is low enough to prevent fermentation.

For bee health and vigor, it's crucial to maintain an environment that supports their natural behaviors and physiological needs. Start by fostering a biodiverse landscape around your hives. Plant a variety of flowers that bloom sequentially throughout the year, such as lavender, sunflowers, and clover, providing a consistent nectar flow. Incorporate water sources like shallow dishes with pebbles, allowing bees to hydrate safely without risk of drowning. Regular hive inspections are vital for monitoring colony health; look for signs of stress or abnormalities in brood patterns that may indicate underlying issues. If pests or diseases do arise, address them promptly using integrated pest management strategies that minimize chemical use and promote natural resilience.

Innovation in beekeeping practices can further enhance hive efficiency and overall productivity. Consider utilizing top-bar hives or Warre hives as alternative designs that may better suit your specific environmental conditions or personal management style. These hives often require less intervention and can promote more natural comb building, which some beekeepers find beneficial for both bees and honey quality. Additionally, technology offers tools that can revolutionize how you manage your apiary. Remote sensors and monitoring systems provide real-time data on temperature, humidity, and hive weight changes, allowing you to make informed decisions without frequent physical inspections. This not only reduces disturbance to the bees but also streamlines your management practices.

Embrace creativity in your approach by experimenting with innovative techniques like rotational grazing for bees—moving hives periodically to different locations within your property or collaborating with local farms to access diverse forage areas throughout the year. This practice not only prevents resource depletion but also exposes your colonies to various floral sources, enhancing honey flavor profiles while supporting pollination in different ecosystems.

By focusing on these key elements—genetic selection, strategic hive management, environmental support, and innovative practices—you can significantly enhance hive productivity and ensure your bees thrive. Each decision made in the apiary reflects a balance between nature's rhythms and human stewardship, fostering an environment where both can flourish harmoniously. As you continue on this path, remain open to learning and adapting, always seeking ways to improve the health and vitality of your bees while contributing positively to the broader ecological landscape they inhabit. Engaging with your hives in this thoughtful manner not only maximizes honey yields but also enriches your understanding and appreciation of these extraordinary creatures.

Resources for Reliable Beekeeping Information

In the ever-evolving world of beekeeping, staying informed and connected with reliable resources is crucial. As someone who has walked the path from novice to seasoned beekeeper, I know the value of having trusted sources at your fingertips. Whether you're troubleshooting hive issues or exploring new techniques, access to quality information can make all the difference in your beekeeping endeavors.

Start by exploring reputable online resources, which offer a wealth of information tailored to both beginners and experienced beekeepers. Websites like the American Beekeeping Federation provide comprehensive guides on everything from hive management to honey harvesting. Their resources for beekeepers section offers articles, webinars, and forums where you can connect with fellow enthusiasts and experts alike (SOURCE 4). Be wary of unverified blogs or forums that might offer conflicting advice; instead, prioritize well-regarded organizations and educational institutions known for their research-based content.

Books remain invaluable companions on your beekeeping journey. Titles like "The Beekeeper's Bible" or "Beekeeping for Dummies" are excellent starting points, offering step-by-step instructions and insights into the intricacies of hive management. These books often come with detailed illustrations and are penned by experienced beekeepers who share their wisdom and anecdotes, making complex concepts accessible and engaging.

Don't underestimate the power of local beekeeping associations. Joining a local group can provide you with a supportive community eager to share knowledge and experiences. These associations often host workshops, field days, and meetings where you can learn firsthand from seasoned beekeepers. Additionally, they may offer mentorship programs that pair you with an experienced beekeeper who can guide you through the nuances of maintaining healthy hives. This kind of hands-on learning is invaluable, as it allows you to see techniques in action and ask questions in real-time.

When evaluating the quality of information, it's important to develop a critical eye. Consider the source's credibility: Is it affiliated with a reputable organization or university? Check for citations or references that back up claims with scientific evidence. Pay attention to the publication date as well; beekeeping practices can evolve rapidly, so accessing the most current information ensures that you're using the best methods available. Cross-referencing multiple sources can also help confirm the accuracy of the information you're relying on.

Continuous learning is the cornerstone of successful beekeeping. The world of bees is dynamic, with new discoveries and innovations emerging regularly. By remaining curious and committed to expanding your knowledge, you'll not only enhance your skills but also contribute positively to your local ecosystem. Attend seminars or conferences when possible; these events offer opportunities to hear from leaders in the field and network with fellow enthusiasts. Online courses or webinars are another convenient way to stay informed without leaving home.

For those looking to delve deeper into specific topics, specialized journals such as "Bee Culture" offer cutting-edge research and articles authored by leading experts in apiculture. Subscriptions to such publications keep you abreast of recent findings and trends, enabling you to fine-tune your practices based on the latest insights.

Interactive Element: Curated Resource List

Create your own curated list of resources that resonate with your beekeeping goals. Include websites, books, local associations, and influential figures in the beekeeping community. Regularly update this list as you discover new sources, ensuring that your knowledge base remains robust and relevant.

In summary, reliable resources are essential companions in your beekeeping journey. They empower you with the knowledge needed to tackle challenges and embrace opportunities within your apiary. Engaging with credible sources, joining local groups, and fostering a spirit of continuous learning enriches your experience and deepens your understanding of these remarkable creatures. As we conclude this chapter on troubleshooting and problem-solving, remember that every challenge presents an opportunity for growth and learning. In the next chapter, we'll explore innovative approaches to hive design, offering new perspectives on enhancing productivity and sustainability within your apiary.

Chapter 11: The Business of Beekeeping

Exploring Honey Sales: From Hive to Market

The scent of honey in the air always takes me back to the bustling days of my childhood, surrounded by my grandfather's beehives. Back then, the magic of extracting honey seemed like a momentous event, with golden liquid flowing from the frames like nature's own elixir. Now, as you enter the realm of honey sales, this transformative process becomes the bridge between your bees and the world eagerly awaiting their sweet offerings.

Harvesting honey begins with careful extraction. Once your frames are full and capped, it's time to uncap them, usually with an uncapping knife or fork. This reveals the honey beneath, ready for collection. The frames are then placed into an extractor, a cylindrical device that spins to utilize centrifugal force, drawing honey out with minimal damage to the comb. Strain the honey through cheesecloth or a fine mesh to remove impurities (Betterbee, n.d.). Afterward, allow it to settle, which lets air bubbles rise for a clearer product. Bottling follows, using sterilized glass jars or food-safe plastic containers to maintain purity and freshness.

Once you have your honey packaged and ready to sell, it's time to explore the best avenues to reach your customers. Farmers' markets provide a personal touch, allowing you to engage directly with buyers and share your passion for beekeeping. Local shops offer another valuable channel; approach grocers or specialty stores that might welcome a locally sourced product. Online platforms also present opportunities; create a simple website or utilize social media to reach a broader audience. Platforms similar to eBay or Etsy can connect you with a niche market seeking unique and artisanal goods (olriley, n.d.).

Setting the right price for your honey is both an art and a science. Consider factors such as production costs, market demand, and quality. Research what similar products sell for in your area and adjust accordingly. Pricing too high might alienate potential buyers, while too low can undervalue your product and affect sustainability. Aim for a balance that reflects quality and assures profitability. Offering different jar sizes can also cater to various budgets and preferences, enhancing customer appeal.

Consistency and quality are paramount in establishing trust and loyalty among your clientele. Each jar should reflect the superior standards you uphold in your apiary practices. Regularly test for moisture content and flavor profiles to ensure consistency. Transparent labeling is crucial; include all necessary information such as net weight, origin, and any certifications if applicable. Customers appreciate clarity and honesty, particularly in artisanal products like honey.

Reflection Section: Documenting Your Honey Journey

To help refine your approach to honey sales, consider maintaining a detailed journal of your experiences. Record each step from extraction to sale—note what works well and where improvements are needed. Reflect on customer feedback and adjust practices accordingly. This not only aids in personal growth but also enhances the quality of your offerings over time.

Navigating the business of beekeeping requires dedication and adaptability. By mastering each phase—from harvesting to market—you'll create a thriving enterprise that celebrates the fruits of your labor while fostering connections between your bee colonies and the community eager to savor their unique gifts.

Value-Added Products: Beeswax and Beyond

Imagine standing in your apiary, the sun casting a warm glow over the hives. You watch your bees dance from flower to flower, each movement a tiny miracle of nature. But the magic of beekeeping doesn't stop at honey. By diversifying your hive's offerings, you can unlock a treasure trove of additional products, each with its own unique market appeal. Beeswax, for instance, is a versatile by-product that can transform your business model. With its natural properties, beeswax opens doors to creating an array of products that cater to both practical uses and luxury markets.

Producing beeswax-based items begins with rendering the wax. Start by collecting cappings and combs left from honey extraction. These should be melted down in a double boiler, allowing impurities to separate and rise. Once melted, strain the wax through cheesecloth or a fine mesh to purify it. Pour the clean wax into molds and let it cool, forming solid blocks ready for crafting. This process not only ensures high-quality wax but also maximizes the yield from each hive component.

With your beeswax prepared, you can explore various product avenues. Candles are a popular choice, celebrated for their slow, clean burn and subtle honey scent. To make them, melt the wax again and pour it into molds with pre-positioned wicks. Lip balms and salves offer another path, combining beeswax with oils like coconut or almond for nourishing skin care. These products appeal to consumers seeking natural alternatives and can be customized with scents or essential oils for added allure.

Beyond these staples, consider venturing into niche market products. Beeswax wraps are gaining traction as sustainable alternatives to plastic food storage. By infusing cotton fabric with beeswax, jojoba oil, and tree resin, you create reusable wraps that are both eco-friendly and functional. Another innovative idea is crafting wood polish from beeswax and oil mixtures, catering to those who value both sustainability and home care. Each of these products highlights the versatility of beeswax and taps into growing trends toward environmentally conscious living.

Collaboration with local artisans offers further opportunity to expand your reach and product line. Partnering with potters or glassblowers can enhance your candles with custom holders or unique jars, creating a distinctive product that stands out in the market. Similarly, teaming up with local soap makers to incorporate beeswax into their products can result in a symbiotic relationship that benefits both parties. These partnerships not only diversify your offerings but also strengthen community ties and support local economies.

Building relationships with local businesses can enhance your brand's visibility and credibility. Approach boutique stores or artisan markets to showcase your products. These venues often attract customers interested in handcrafted goods and provide exposure to buyers who appreciate quality craftsmanship. Hosting workshops or demonstrations can further engage potential customers, offering them a glimpse into the meticulous process behind each product and fostering a deeper connection to your brand.

To ensure success in these ventures, maintain a focus on quality and innovation. Each product should embody the same level of care and dedication you invest in your beekeeping practices. Consistency in production and presentation builds trust with customers, encouraging repeat business and word-of-mouth referrals. Stay attuned to market trends and customer feedback, adapting your offerings as needed to meet evolving demands.

In the realm of value-added products, creativity knows no bounds. By leveraging the full potential of your hives, you not only enhance profitability but also contribute to sustainable practices that resonate with today's conscientious consumers. As you explore these possibilities, remember that each new venture reflects not just an expansion of your business but an extension of the harmonious relationship between you, your bees, and the world around you.

Marketing Your Beekeeping Products

In the bustling world of beekeeping, where honey glistens like liquid gold and beeswax is molded into enchanting forms, branding emerges as a powerful tool. Branding isn't just about creating a catchy name or designing an attractive logo; it's about crafting a story that resonates with your audience. Consider the values you wish to convey—whether it's sustainability, purity, or local craftsmanship—and weave these into your brand narrative. This story should be reflected in every interaction customers have with your product, from the packaging design that captures their eyes to the tasting notes that delight their palates. Effective branding differentiates your products in a crowded market, making them memorable and desirable. Emphasize authenticity and let the passion for your craft shine through every element of your brand.

As the digital age continues to expand its reach, building an online presence becomes increasingly vital for spreading your brand's message. Start by creating a professional website that not only showcases your products but also tells your unique story. Use high-quality images and vibrant descriptions to bring your offerings to life. Engage with social media platforms like Instagram and Facebook where visual content thrives. Regular posts about the beekeeping process, behind-the-scenes looks at production, or even stories about the bees themselves can captivate and educate your audience. Consider blogging to share insights, tips, and the latest trends in beekeeping, establishing yourself as an authority in the field. Engage followers through interactive content like polls or live Q&A sessions, fostering a sense of community and connection.

Customer engagement doesn't end with getting your product into buyers' hands; it requires ongoing interaction to build long-term relationships. Encourage feedback by asking customers to share their experiences and opinions. This input not only helps you improve your products but also makes customers feel valued and heard. Offering loyalty programs or exclusive discounts can incentivize repeat purchases, while personalized communication—such as thank-you notes or birthday messages—adds a personal touch that strengthens bonds. Hosting events like honey tastings or beekeeping workshops can also draw interest and establish deeper connections with your audience. Remember, engaged customers are more likely to become advocates for your brand, spreading word-of-mouth recommendations that are invaluable for growth.

Listening to customer feedback is crucial for product development and refinement. Pay attention to what consumers appreciate and where they see room for improvement. This information provides valuable insights into market trends and helps guide decision-making for new products or enhancements. Perhaps customers express a desire for smaller honey jars or suggest experimenting with new flavors—such feedback is a goldmine for innovation. Implementing changes based on customer suggestions demonstrates your responsiveness and commitment to satisfaction. Moreover, it fosters loyalty by ensuring that your offerings align with their evolving preferences and expectations.

To further capitalize on these insights, consider implementing regular surveys or feedback forms where customers can freely express their thoughts. Analyze this data to identify patterns and areas of opportunity. For example, if a significant number of responses indicate interest in eco-friendly packaging, exploring sustainable materials could set you apart from competitors while meeting consumer demand. Similarly, if customers praise a particular product aspect, such as its rich flavor or smooth texture, highlight these attributes in marketing efforts to reinforce positive perceptions. Engaging customers in this way not only enhances your products but also cultivates a sense of ownership among them.

As you navigate the multifaceted realm of marketing for your beekeeping business, remember that success lies in authenticity, engagement, and adaptability. Your brand should reflect the passion and dedication you pour into your craft, resonating with those who appreciate quality and care. By leveraging digital tools, fostering meaningful connections, and valuing customer input, you can create a thriving enterprise that delights consumers while honoring the bees at its heart.

Legal Considerations for Selling Honey

As you delve into the fascinating, albeit intricate world of selling honey from your thriving hives, understanding the legal landscape becomes an indispensable part of your business journey, ensuring your enterprise is not only productive but also sustainable. The regulatory requirements for honey sales can vary significantly depending on your geographic location, making it essential to intricately familiarize yourself with the specific standards applicable to your state, region, or even municipality. This variation in legal stipulations underscores the importance of comprehensive research and due diligence. These ever-important legal standards often encompass diverse areas such as labeling, safety inspections, and quality assurance. These ensure that your honey meets both consumer expectations and stringent health regulations, laying a robust foundation for trust and credibility. For instance, many regions require that honey be labeled with specific, detail-oriented information such as its origin, weight, and any additives. This transparency is not merely a legal compulsion but rather a strategic tool to fortify consumer confidence, clearly delineating your commitment to quality and openness.

Navigating the intricate process of obtaining necessary licenses and permits might seem daunting and overwhelming at first glance, but it is undeniably a crucial step in legitimizing your honey sales operation. Begin by meticulously researching your local government's health department or agricultural extension office. They typically provide a comprehensive set of guidelines and resources regarding permits you might need and the intricacies of applying for them. Interestingly, some areas might exhibit leniency by allowing small-scale sales without extensive permits under burgeoning Cottage Food laws, while others might demand more rigorous oversight and stringent compliance. Therefore, it's vital to understand these distinctions varying by jurisdiction and ensure you meet all legal obligations to sidestep potential fines or business interruptions. Meticulous and organized record-keeping of all permits is paramount, along with timely renewals, to maintain unbroken compliance with local laws and regulations.

Liability insurance emerges as another vital consideration for anyone engaging in the sale of food products like honey. This insurance acts as a protective shield for your business from potential legal claims related to product safety or other issues that could unexpectedly arise from the consumption of your honey. While you strive diligently for the highest quality in every jar you produce, having liability coverage offers an invaluable layer of peace of mind, safeguarding your financial interests against unforeseen and potentially damaging circumstances. Consult with a seasoned insurance broker who specializes in small businesses or agricultural enterprises to find a policy uniquely tailored to suit your specific needs without overwhelming or unduly stretching your budget.

When it comes to adeptly navigating these legal challenges, seeking professional guidance can truly make all the difference in the world. Consider reaching out to resources such as local business development centers or well-established beekeeping associations that may offer legally sound advice specifically tailored to beekeepers. These organizations often provide enriching workshops, informative seminars, or personalized one-on-one consultations to help you grasp the intricate details of running a beekeeping business efficiently and in accordance with the law. Additionally, collaborating with fellow beekeepers can offer invaluable insights and shared experiences, transforming the process into something less intimidating and more manageable, fostering a supportive community ethos.

As you meticulously integrate these legal considerations into your ever-evolving business model, remember that each step taken towards compliance strengthens your operation's foundation. These efforts ensure that you're not only aligned with regulations but also enhance your credibility as a responsible producer in the discerning eyes of your esteemed customers and peers. By adhering to legal standards, obtaining all the appropriate licenses, securing robust liability insurance, and seeking expert advice, you astutely position your beekeeping enterprise for sustained long-term success and stability.

In summary, understanding and meticulously adhering to the encompassing legal framework surrounding honey sales is paramount for maintaining a reputable and thriving business. It ensures that you can focus on what you genuinely love—producing excellent honey—while resting assured that your operations are secure and legally sound, sealed with an assurance of quality and integrity. As we elegantly conclude this chapter on the intricate business aspects of beekeeping, we seamlessly transition into exploring future trends in apiculture, where stimulating innovation meets cherished tradition in shaping the promising future of beekeeping practices and transformative technology.

Chapter 12: The Future of Beekeeping

Technological Advances in Beekeeping

Imagine a world where your beehive communicates with you, sharing insights about its health and productivity without needing to crack it open. This is not a distant dream but an emerging reality. Modern technology is revolutionizing traditional beekeeping, offering tools that make the practice more efficient and insightful. With technology, the beekeeping landscape is evolving rapidly, bringing a wealth of advancements that promise to change how you interact with your buzzing companions. The integration of technology into hive management is transforming beekeeping practices, making it both an art and a science.

At the forefront of this transformation are smart beehives. These hives, equipped with sensors, provide real-time data on a variety of factors such as temperature, humidity, and hive weight. By monitoring these parameters, smart hives allow you to gain insights into the internal conditions of your colony without the need for frequent physical inspections. This remote monitoring capability not only saves time but also enables early detection of potential issues like pest infestations or environmental stressors. Thus, smart beehives support sustainable beekeeping by ensuring honeybee vitality (Smart Beehives: Revolutionizing Beekeeping Practices).

Automation in beekeeping is another leap forward. It streamlines tasks that were once labor-intensive and time-consuming. Automated systems can handle hive inspections, honey extraction, and even pest control with minimal human intervention. For instance, automatic honey extractors spin frames at the optimal speed to ensure efficient honey harvesting without damaging the combs. By reducing manual labor, automation allows you to focus on strategic decisions that enhance your apiary's productivity and health. The efficiency gained through automation not only boosts productivity but also frees up valuable time for you to enjoy other aspects of beekeeping.

Artificial intelligence (AI) is making its mark in this field by enhancing decision-making processes. AI algorithms can analyze data collected from smart hives, providing predictions and recommendations based on patterns and trends. For example, AI can help forecast swarming behavior by analyzing bee activity and environmental conditions. It can also suggest optimal times for feeding or harvesting based on past data. This kind of insight was once the domain of seasoned beekeepers with years of experience. Now, AI offers these expert-level insights to anyone willing to embrace technology, democratizing access to professional-grade beekeeping strategies.

The horizon of beekeeping technology is vast and promising. Innovations like drone-assisted hive inspections are in development, offering non-invasive ways to assess hive health from above. These drones can capture high-resolution images and videos, providing a bird's-eye view of your apiary. Additionally, advancements in blockchain technology are being explored for honey authentication and traceability. This could revolutionize how honey is marketed and sold by ensuring transparency and trust in the supply chain. Such cutting-edge technologies not only enhance productivity but also address concerns about product authenticity and environmental impact.

Interactive Element: Tech-Enhanced Beekeeping Journal

Consider starting a digital beekeeping journal to track your hive's data over time. Document observations from your smart hive, noting changes in temperature or humidity and any corresponding hive behaviors or outcomes. This practice will help you recognize patterns and make informed decisions based on historical data. As technology evolves, keeping a digital record will become even more valuable, offering a comprehensive picture of your beekeeping journey.

By embracing these technological advances, you stand at the forefront of a new era in beekeeping. The fusion of traditional wisdom with modern innovation offers endless possibilities for enhancing your practice while contributing to broader ecological goals. As technology continues to evolve, so too will the opportunities for growth and learning within the world of beekeeping.

The Role of Beekeeping in Conservation Efforts

Beekeeping extends beyond the simple act of tending to hives. It plays a crucial role in preserving biodiversity and maintaining delicate ecosystems. As bees flit from flower to flower, they perform pollination, a vital process that sustains plant life and, in turn, the wildlife that depends on those plants. This intricate dance of life ensures that ecosystems remain robust and resilient. By fostering healthy bee populations, beekeeping contributes significantly to the conservation of biodiversity. This practice not only supports honeybees but also creates environments where wild bees and other pollinators can thrive, helping to stabilize ecosystems that are increasingly under threat from human activities and climate change.

Numerous initiatives around the globe leverage beekeeping as a tool for ecological restoration. In areas where natural habitats have been degraded or lost, projects use beekeeping to rejuvenate local flora and fauna. For example, some conservation programs introduce managed bees into regions where natural pollinators have dwindled due to environmental stressors. These bees help revive native plant species by ensuring they receive the pollination required for reproduction. Over time, this leads to increased plant diversity, which attracts other wildlife back to the area, thus restoring ecological balance. Such projects highlight the power of beekeeping to kickstart restoration efforts and bring life back to struggling ecosystems.

Collaboration between beekeepers and conservation organizations has become increasingly common as both parties recognize the mutual benefits of working together. Conservation groups provide resources and guidance to beekeepers, helping them adopt practices that enhance sustainability. Meanwhile, beekeepers offer valuable insights into bee behavior and hive management, contributing to broader environmental goals. These partnerships often result in innovative strategies that promote biodiversity and sustainable practices. For instance, joint efforts might focus on planting bee-friendly flora in urban areas to support pollinators or developing community gardens that serve as educational hubs for sustainable agriculture. Through these collaborations, beekeepers and conservationists amplify their impact on environmental preservation.

Managed beekeeping also plays a pivotal role in supporting endangered bee species. While honeybees are often the focus, many wild bee populations face significant threats from habitat loss, pesticides, and disease. By maintaining healthy honeybee colonies, beekeepers provide indirect support to wild bees. Managed colonies can serve as reservoirs of healthy genetics that may bolster wild populations through cross-pollination. Additionally, initiatives aimed at protecting honeybees often benefit other bee species by raising awareness about pollinator decline and encouraging more sustainable land-use practices. By acting as stewards of bee health and diversity, beekeepers contribute to broader efforts to protect all pollinators from extinction.

Beekeeping's contribution to conservation is not limited to rural or natural settings; it holds potential even in urban environments. City-based beekeeping initiatives have emerged as a novel way to enhance urban biodiversity. Rooftop hives in cities create pockets of green in concrete jungles, providing essential foraging opportunities for bees amidst urban sprawl. These bees help pollinate urban gardens and parks, increasing plant diversity within cityscapes. Moreover, urban beekeeping projects often engage local communities, raising awareness about pollinator health and inspiring city dwellers to take part in conservation efforts. By integrating nature into urban spaces through beekeeping, cities become more sustainable and livable for both people and wildlife.

Reflecting on these aspects of beekeeping reveals its multifaceted role in conservation efforts worldwide. The practice not only safeguards pollinators but also fosters resilient ecosystems that support a wide range of biodiversity. As you consider your involvement in beekeeping, think about how your efforts contribute to these larger environmental goals. Whether you're cultivating a small backyard apiary or participating in a community beekeeping project, each action you take plays a part in preserving the planet's precious biodiversity. The story of beekeeping is one of collaboration between humans and nature—a narrative where each participant has the power to make a meaningful difference in conserving the world we share.

Educating the Next Generation of Beekeepers

Involving young people in beekeeping is not just about securing the future of this age-old practice; it's about fostering a deeper connection between the next generation and the environment. Youth engagement in beekeeping instills a sense of responsibility and awareness about the crucial role bees play in our ecosystems. As these young minds discover the intricacies of bee life, they develop an appreciation for biodiversity that transcends mere academic knowledge. Through hands-on experience, they learn about ecology, agriculture, and sustainability, equipping them with skills and values that are vital for future environmental stewardship.

Various educational programs have successfully introduced beekeeping to young audiences, tapping into their innate curiosity and enthusiasm. For instance, school garden initiatives often include beekeeping as part of their curriculum, allowing students to observe bees in action and learn about their symbiotic relationship with plants. These programs provide students with the opportunity to participate in hive management, honey extraction, and even bee-friendly gardening. By engaging students in practical activities, they gain firsthand experience and a deeper understanding of the vital role bees play in food production and environmental health.

The role of technology in beekeeping education cannot be overlooked. Digital tools have transformed how young people learn about bees, making the subject more accessible and engaging. Virtual reality (VR) experiences allow students to explore the inside of a hive without leaving their classroom, providing an immersive learning experience that captivates their imagination. Online platforms also offer interactive lessons, quizzes, and videos that illustrate complex concepts in a digestible format. By integrating technology into beekeeping education, we can reach a wider audience and inspire a new generation to take an interest in this important practice.

Mentoring young beekeepers is another crucial aspect of fostering interest and expertise in beekeeping. Experienced beekeepers play a vital role in guiding newcomers, offering wisdom and support as they navigate the challenges of hive management. To effectively mentor young beekeepers, it's important to foster an environment of patience and encouragement. Share your stories and insights, highlighting both successes and lessons learned from mistakes. Encourage questions and curiosity, allowing young beekeepers to explore different approaches and develop their own understanding of beekeeping.

Providing hands-on experiences is invaluable for young learners. Invite them to participate in hive inspections, explaining each step and its purpose. Show them how to handle bees safely and teach them to recognize signs of healthy hives versus those that may need attention. Encourage them to observe bee behavior closely, noting changes that might indicate issues within the colony. Hands-on learning not only builds confidence but also instills a sense of accomplishment as young beekeepers see their efforts contribute to thriving hives.

Another strategy for mentoring is facilitating networking opportunities with other young beekeepers. Organize local meet-ups or online forums where they can share experiences, ask questions, and learn from one another. Creating a community of young beekeepers fosters collaboration and camaraderie, helping them feel connected to a larger movement dedicated to preserving pollinators. As they exchange ideas and insights, they develop a broader perspective on beekeeping practices and their impact on the environment.

To further support young beekeepers, consider providing access to resources such as books, videos, or workshops tailored to their learning level. These resources should cover foundational topics like bee anatomy, hive management basics, and bee-friendly gardening practices. As they grow more confident in their abilities, encourage exploration into advanced topics like queen rearing or honey harvesting techniques. Gradually expanding their knowledge base keeps them engaged and motivated to continue their journey into beekeeping.

Incorporating fun activities into the learning process can also enhance engagement among young beekeepers. Host honey-tasting events where they can sample different varieties of honey and learn about flavor profiles influenced by floral sources. Organize bee-themed art projects or storytelling sessions where they can express their creativity while reinforcing their understanding of bees' ecological importance. These activities make learning enjoyable while reinforcing key concepts through playful exploration.

By investing time and effort into educating the next generation of beekeepers, we ensure that this vital practice continues to thrive for years to come. As these young individuals grow into knowledgeable stewards of the environment, they carry forward a legacy that supports biodiversity conservation and sustainable agriculture practices worldwide. Through education and mentorship, we empower them with tools needed not just for successful hive management but also for contributing positively toward a healthier planet overall—a mission that matters today more than ever before.

The Global Impact of Beekeeping Practices

The influence of beekeeping on global agriculture cannot be overstated. Bees are responsible for pollinating a vast majority of the world's crops, making them indispensable to food security and agricultural productivity. From almond orchards in California to sunflower fields in Ukraine, the work of bees ensures that plants reproduce, leading to bountiful harvests. This pollination process boosts crop yields and enhances the quality of produce, providing vital nutrients for millions worldwide. Without bees, the diversity of our diet would diminish drastically, affecting everything from fruits and vegetables to nuts and oils. Beekeeping, therefore, plays a critical role in sustaining global food supplies and supporting the livelihoods of countless farmers.

Despite its importance, beekeeping faces numerous challenges across the globe. Climate change stands at the forefront, altering weather patterns and disrupting flowering cycles. This affects the availability of forage for bees, sometimes leading to starvation or weakened colonies. Pesticide use, particularly in intensive farming regions, poses another significant threat. These chemicals can be toxic to bees, leading to declines in bee populations. Furthermore, diseases and pests such as Varroa mites continue to plague hives worldwide. These issues require constant vigilance and innovative solutions from beekeepers to ensure their colonies remain healthy and productive amidst these adversities.

In response to these challenges, international collaborations in beekeeping research have gained momentum. Researchers and beekeepers from different countries are joining forces to address common issues that transcend borders. For instance, global partnerships focus on developing mite-resistant bee strains or organic treatment methods that can be adopted worldwide. Additionally, shared research on habitat restoration provides insights into creating environments where bees can thrive despite urbanization and habitat destruction. These collaborative efforts not only enhance our understanding of beekeeping challenges but also foster a sense of community among beekeepers across continents, united by a shared goal to protect these vital pollinators.

Culturally, beekeeping holds significant meaning in various regions around the world. In many African countries, beekeeping is more than an agricultural practice; it's a cultural tradition passed down through generations. Traditional methods often emphasize natural hive construction and sustainable harvesting techniques that align with local ecosystems. In Eastern Europe, honey is not just a sweetener but a staple in traditional recipes and medicinal remedies. Similarly, indigenous communities in Latin America have practiced beekeeping for centuries, using beeswax for spiritual ceremonies and honey as a symbol of abundance. These diverse cultural practices highlight the deep connection between humans and bees, showcasing how beekeeping enriches cultural heritage while supporting environmental sustainability.

In Asia, particularly in China and India, large-scale commercial beekeeping operations reflect the growing demand for honey and other bee products. However, this scale presents its own set of challenges, such as maintaining genetic diversity among bee populations and managing large apiaries sustainably. Meanwhile, in Western countries like the United States and Australia, backyard beekeeping has surged in popularity as people seek to reconnect with nature and contribute to local ecosystems. This rise in small-scale beekeeping reflects a broader trend towards sustainability and environmental stewardship among individuals who recognize the importance of bees beyond their economic value.

The global impact of beekeeping practices underscores the interconnectedness of our world. The health of bee populations influences not only local ecosystems but also international food security and biodiversity. As you engage with beekeeping, consider how your efforts contribute to this larger picture. By implementing sustainable practices and advocating for pollinator protection, you join a global movement dedicated to preserving the delicate balance of our planet's ecosystems.

As we conclude this chapter on the future of beekeeping, it's clear that this practice holds immense potential for positive impact on both local and global scales. By adopting innovative techniques and fostering collaborations across borders, we can overcome challenges and ensure that bees continue to thrive for generations to come. Looking ahead, the next chapter will explore practical steps for incorporating sustainable practices into your daily beekeeping routine, empowering you to make a meaningful difference in your own backyard and beyond.

Conclusion

As we reach the end of our journey together, I hope this book has served as a guiding light on your beekeeping path. We've explored the intricacies of bee behavior, the nuts and bolts of hive setup, and the nuanced art of hive management. Each chapter aimed to equip you with both the practical skills and the deeper appreciation necessary to nurture a thriving backyard apiary. We've delved into the seasonal rhythms of beekeeping, emphasizing how each season offers unique challenges and opportunities for growth. Through sustainable practices, you can ensure that your bees not only survive but flourish, contributing positively to the ecosystem.

The role of bees in garden ecosystems cannot be overstated. These small creatures are mighty pollinators, essential for the health and productivity of our plants. By integrating bees into your garden, you're not just adding a hive; you're creating a vibrant, living tapestry that supports biodiversity and ecological balance. Your garden becomes a sanctuary, not just for bees, but for a host of other creatures that depend on their pollination.

As you reflect on the insights shared in this book, remember the core lessons: understanding bee behavior, embracing ethical and sustainable practices, and effectively managing your hives through the seasons. These principles form the foundation of successful beekeeping and will guide you as you continue your journey. I encourage you to keep a beekeeping journal, documenting your experiences, challenges, and triumphs. This practice not only tracks your progress but also deepens your understanding and connection to your bees.

Beekeeping is not a solitary endeavor. It thrives on community and shared knowledge. I urge you to connect with fellow beekeepers, whether through local clubs or online forums. These communities offer invaluable support, fresh ideas, and camaraderie. Engaging with others enriches your experience and strengthens the beekeeping community as a whole.

Continued learning is vital in beekeeping. The field is ever-evolving, with new research and innovations continually emerging. Stay curious and seek out new information. Attend workshops, read the latest studies, and explore new techniques. This commitment to learning will enhance your skills and ensure your apiary remains healthy and productive.

I invite you to take action, applying the knowledge you've gained to improve your hives and contribute to ecological conservation. Educate others about the importance of bees and inspire them to take up beekeeping or support pollinator-friendly practices. Each step you take contributes to a larger movement toward sustainability and environmental stewardship.

Thank you for choosing this book as your guide. Your dedication to beekeeping and sustainable living is commendable. By supporting bee populations, you play a crucial role in preserving biodiversity and ensuring the health of our planet.

Looking to the future, I am filled with hope. The collective efforts of beekeepers like you are making a difference. Together, we can create a world where bees thrive, gardens flourish, and ecosystems remain resilient. Your commitment is part of a broader vision for a sustainable future, one where humans and nature coexist harmoniously.

With these thoughts, I leave you informed, inspired, and ready to continue your beekeeping journey with renewed enthusiasm. May your hives buzz with life, and may your gardens bloom with the fruits of your labor.

References

- *Understanding The Role Of The Queen Bee In A Colony* https://www.ecrotek.com.au/blogs/articles/understanding-the-role-of-the-queen-bee-in-a-colony#:~:text=The%20queen%20controls%20the%20population,the%20larger%20males%20are%20drones. text=The%20average%20queen%20bee%20will%20live%20from%20two%20to%20five%20years.

- *Social signal learning of the waggle dance in honey bees* https://www.science.org/doi/10.1126/science.ade1702

- *Urban Beekeeping Guide: Benefits, Practices, & Equipment.* https://www.ecobeeremoval.com/blog/the-complete-guide-to-urban-beekeeping

- *Comparison of Russian and Italian Honey Bees* https://content.ces.ncsu.edu/comparison-of-russian-and-italian-honey-bees

- *Varroosis - USDA ARS* https://www.ars.usda.gov/pacific-west-area/tucson-az/carl-hayden-bee-research-center/research/varroa/varroosis/#:~:text=PMS%20encompasses%20a%20range%20of,decreasing%20adult%20population%2C%20bees%20with

- *Methods to Control Varroa Mites: An Integrated Pest ...* https://extension.psu.edu/methods-to-control-varroa-mites-an-integrated-pest-management-approach

- *Seasonal Beekeeping Checklists: Spring and Summer* https://nodglobal.com/seasonal-beekeeping-checklists-spring-and-summer/

- *Beehive Ventilation: How to Vent Your Hive* https://carolinahoneybees.com/beehive-ventilation/

- *How to Feed Bees During Winter* https://www.twohiveshoney.com/feeding-bees-in-winter/?srsltid=AfmBOoqRBQtMr2oZrFkWX0Uo_KD8uEd9K7GBkQM-ZEQXWnUyJDWZtUE-

- *Quick Tips for the First Hive Inspection After Winter* https://www.betterbee.com/instructions-and-resources/first-inspection-of-the-season.asp?srsltid=AfmBOordx4tybWqzZm9iy40PCCcuSchDl9ykrIKzwZenILNfCMeVejOf

- *When & How-To Harvest & Extract Honey* https://talkingwithbees.com/beekeeping-how-to-guides/harvesting-honey

- *Fall management* https://canr.udel.edu/maarec/wp-content/uploads/sites/18/2010/03/FALL_MGM.pdf

- *Why are bees so important for biodiversity?* https://www.zurich.com/media/magazine/2023/why-are-bees-so-important-for-biodiversity

- *Pollinator-Friendly Native Plant Lists* https://xerces.org/pollinator-conservation/pollinator-friendly-plant-lists

- *Urban Beekeeping: Honey Havens in Concrete Jungles* https://happyeconews.com/urban-beekeeping/#:~:text=Paris%2C%20for%20example%2C%20has%20become,point%20of%20pride%20for%20Parisians.

- *Bee Behaviour During Foraging - Apiculture Factsheet* https://www2.gov.bc.ca/assets/gov/farming-natural-resources-and-industry/agriculture-and-seafood/animal-and-crops/animal-production/bee-assets/api_fs111.pdf

- *Honey Bee Swarm Prevention Tactics* https://www.betterbee.com/instructions-and-resources/what-works-to-prevent-swarming.asp?srsltid=AfmBOornCtFctkh-SDGmia6OWZvPha-pUYYpTS_O8TP15BasX8mwKQs6E

- *Queen Rearing Methods and Equipment | Beekeeping ...* https://www.dadant.com/learn/queen-rearing-methods-and-equipment/

- *Expanding your apiary* https://www.honeyflow.com/blogs/livestreams/expanding-your-apiary-210120?srsltid=AfmBOopMdZt65J8fwqcXT5S622HbVfnhG0AKiyl3YaXdlgVav7npY-8q

- *A Quick Reference Guide to Honey Bee Parasites, Pests, ...* https://extension.psu.edu/a-quick-reference-guide-to-honey-bee-parasites-pests-predators-and-diseases

- *How to Choose Protective Beekeeping Gear* https://www.betterbee.com/instructions-and-resources/protective-beekeeping-gear.asp?srsltid=AfmBOoqr3-4aHqPMO-nxrcZpoagu4dMgseKs-Dfuf5cNGmfkc6fQWt6e-

- *Stings - Beekeeping Resources - Bee Program - UGA* https://bees.caes.uga.edu/beekeeping-resources/getting-started-topics/getting-started-stings.html#:~:text=You%20can%20greatly%20reduce%20stinging,and%20receive%20very%20few%20stings.

- *Beekeeping Laws and Regulations* https://cambp.ucdavis.edu/knowledge-base/legal

- *Ethical Beekeeping: Our Sustainable Practices - Manukora* https://manukora.com/blogs/honey-guide/ethical-beekeeping#:~:text=Ethical%20beekeepers%20avoid%20using%20pesticides,focus%20on%20supporting%20local%20ecosystems.

- *How To Build a Beehive: A DIY Guide* https://todayshomeowner.com/lawn-garden/guides/how-to-build-a-beehive/

- *Cheapest hive equipment supplier : r/Beekeeping* https://www.reddit.com/r/Beekeeping/comments/1bpgklu/cheapest_hive_equipment_supplier/

- *Beekeeping On A Budget* https://www.beeculture.com/beekeeping-on-a-budget/

- *Grant Opportunities* https://www.pollinator.org/grants

- *How does organic farming benefit honey bees? - Phys.org* https://phys.org/news/2024-08-farming-benefit-honey-bees.html#:~:text=Organic%20farming%20and%20flower%20strips,are%20less%20exposed%20to%20pesticides.

- *Responsible Practices for Sustainable Hives* https://pollinatorpioneers.org.uk/the-ethical-beekeeper-responsible-practices-for-sustainable-hives/

- *Sustainable Beekeeping Practices for the Environment* https://www.beekeepinggear.com.au/blogs/article/sustainable-beekeeping-reduce-environmental-impact?srsltid=AfmBOopS_oSZ1Y2PUU7Huy2AVf1Tiil2cjLA5Mv4wkUDxx_h5exH2sxS

- *The Secret Life of Beekeepers* https://countryroadsmagazine.com/outdoors/knowing-nature/the-secret-life-of-beekeepers/

- *Beekeeping with Kids* https://www.perfectbee.com/learn-about-bees/about-beekeeping/beekeeping-with-kids

- *Beekeeping 101* https://extension.psu.edu/beekeeping-101

- *The Benefits of Joining a Beekeeping Club* https://www.keepingbackyardbees.com/benefits-of-joining-a-beekeeping-club-zbwz1903zsau/

- *Honey bee pests and diseases* https://agriculture.vic.gov.au/biosecurity/animal-diseases/honey-bee-pests-and-diseases

- *Climate Change Threatens Honey Bee Colonies* https://www.technologynetworks.com/applied-sciences/news/climate-change-threatens-honey-bee-colonies-385151

- *Maximizing Honey Production and Heating Honey* https://extension.msstate.edu/sites/default/files/publications/publications/p3382.pdf

- *Resources for Beekeepers* https://abfnet.org/resources-for-beekeepers/

- *How to Extract Honey from Bee Hives - Betterbee* https://www.betterbee.com/instructions-and-resources/how-to-extract-honey.asp#:~:text=You%20can%20strain%20using%20cheese-cloth,your%20filtering%20and%20packaging%20process.

- *Online websites or apps for selling honey locally?* https://beekeepingforum.co.uk/threads/online-websites-or-apps-for-selling-honey-locally.42773/

- *How to Sell Your Hive's Honey - A state by state guide* https://localhoneyfinder.org/Selling_Honey_In_Your_State.php

- *Value-added products from beekeeping. Chapter 1.* https://www.fao.org/4/w0076e/w0076e03.htm

- *Smart Beehives: Revolutionizing Beekeeping Practices* https://www.planetbee.org/post/smart-beehives-revolutionizing-beekeeping-practices

- *Challenging the sustainability of urban beekeeping using ...* https://www.nature.com/articles/s42949-021-00046-6

- *Kids and Bees* https://abfnet.org/kids-and-bees/

- *Celebrating Indigenous Beekeeping Practices on World ...* https://www.culturalsurvival.org/news/celebrating-indigenous-beekeeping-practices-world-bee-day

Also By

The Quick Guide to Self-Help: Practical strategies for Personal Growth

The Little Book of Self-Help: Sorting out the Big Questions

The Bipolar Journey

Practical Wellness Collection: The Quick Guide, the Little Book, The Bipolar Journey

Marriage: The Hitch and the Glitch of Wedded Bliss

On Being a Woman: Trials, Tribulations and Triumphs

Ageless Aging; Embrace Aging with Purpose

The Dark Web and Scams

Technology and Future Trends: Reflections on the Future of Technology and Society

Cracks in the Foundation: Dealing with Doubt in the Your Faith

Nature's Pharmacy: Growing and Using Medicinal Plants

https://ivettesmithbooks.com/